SCEPTICISM INC.

D1177126

To my parents; Nancy and Malcolm,
To Janette, Julie, Justine, Jenny and Julie,
And my agents Gill Coleridge and Harriet Gugenheim.

SCEPTICISM INC.

Bo Fowler

BLOOMSBURY

Copyright © 1998 by Bo Fowler

All rights reserved. No part of this book may be used or
reproduced in any manner whatsoever without written
permission except in the case of brief quotations embodied
in critical articles or reviews. For information address
Bloomsbury Publishing, 175 Fifth Avenue, New York, N.Y. 10010.

Published by Bloomsbury Publishing, New York and London.
Distributed to the trade by St. Martin's Press

First published in Great Britain 1998 by
Jonathan Cape
Random House

A CIP catalogue record for this book
is available from the Library of Congress

ISBN 1–58234–072–2

First U.S. Edition 1999
10 9 8 7 6 5 4 3 2 1

Typeset by Palimpsest Book Production Limited,
Polmont, Stirlingshire, Scotland
Printed in the United States of America by
R.R. Donnelley & Sons Company,
Harrisonburg, Virginia

'*Machinery is the new Messiah.*'
Henry Ford

'*There is not enough religion in the world
even to destroy religions.*'
Friedrich Nietzsche

'*Why do you torture your poor reason for insight
into the riddle of eternity?*'
Horace

ACKNOWLEDGEMENTS

This message from space, this long and winding electromagnetic transmission, broadcast on the wavelength of twenty-one centimetres and due to arrive on Earth ten years from now (sometime in the 221st century), would not have been possible without the help of many people and electrical appliances – too many to name here. However, I must express my heartfelt gratitude and love to Kitty Fitzgerald for introducing me to the universe, giving me my sex and giving me a piece of helpful advice. I must also thank ShopALot, the third largest chain of supermarket stores in Europe, for whom I worked. I also wish to acknowledge my obvious debt to George Milles Jr, the second wealthiest man ever to live and the inventor of the Infinity Chip. I would also like to thank NASA and the fifteen thousand people that helped place me in low Earth orbit. I feel I am a brother to each and every one of you.

Of course all of these people are long since dead. Most perished in the Great Mania.

Edgar Malroy is also dead. He died at the end of the Holy War which took place a little while after the Great Mania.

Edgar Malroy was the closest friend I ever had on Earth.

So I once bet £500,000 that God existed; doesn't everyone make at least one mistake?

PROLOGUE

Florida was the largest producer of tangerines in the world.

Production in the late 1990s reached twenty million boxes annually.

Orange City, a town in the south of Florida, had a population in 1998 of just 2,795.

One person who lived in Orange City at that time and had occasional involvement with the tangerine business was Daphne Stephenson.

Daphne Stephenson was a check-out girl in one of Orange City's two supermarkets that had been owned by the Davies family for nearly forty years.

Daphne Stephenson had gone to school with Bob Davies. Bob Davies inherited the two supermarkets in Orange City in 1997.

They had necked once behind the gym, Daphne Stephenson and Bob Davies, in their youth. Daphne's jaw would dislocate.

Pop.

Three times she had to break away from Bob Davies' amorous embrace and push her jaw back into place with two fingers.

Daphne Stephenson sometimes had epileptic fits too.

So did St Antony, the patron saint of skin rashes. So did Jesus Christ. So did Mohammed the prophet.

On the 16th of June 1998 she had a fit while at work. Bob Davies didn't phone for an ambulance. He called over his priest who, as providence would have it, was shopping in the frozen meats section.

The priest, a man by the name of Stephen L. Jones, had a

theological degree from Xenophobe Bible School in Portland, Oregon, where the most exciting thing to do on a Saturday night was to listen to Professor Watmough snoring, in the vain hope that he would utter something interesting in his sleep. Stephen L. Jones decided that Daphne Stephenson was possessed by a devil. A medium sort of devil. He proposed a tried and tested treatment.

First, prayers were uttered as Daphne Stephenson, foaming and shaking wildly, fell off her check-out seat.

The till was closed.

Daphne's jaw went pop.

As Daphne's condition deteriorated, more drastic measures were taken.

The priest rolled up his sleeves and hit her about the body with a frozen ostrich leg.

The post-mortem examination of Daphne Stephenson's body showed that she had suffered four broken ribs, a broken arm and a fractured skull. It was the fractured skull that killed her.

The priest left with four bags of shopping. Daphne Stephenson's body was hidden in the supermarket deep freeze by Bob Davies.

The till was opened.

The police found the body. They got eye-witness accounts. They went to arrest the priest. But by then the priest and his followers, including Bob Davies, the manager of the supermarket, had barricaded themselves inside their church. As people do.

It was a little church, built on a small knoll and surrounded by a white painted fence and poplar trees. There were thirty-five different species of wild flower growing on the grass around the church. Although no one had ever counted them.

Inside the church huddled twenty-six people who had decided to dedicate the rest of their lives to protecting Stephen L. Jones, the priest who was becoming known on the TV and in the papers as the Ostrich Preacher. Most of the twenty-six faithful were tangerine pickers or retired tangerine pickers or would-be tangerine pickers. In fact just about everyone huddled in the church had in some way or other occasional involvement with the tangerine business.

They also somehow had guns. Big old Chinese guns.

When the police arrived they were greeted with a hail of fire. They had expected this. The police had got used to being greeted with a hail of gunfire when they went to churches on business, what with it being nearly the end of the millennium. The holy were trigger-happy.

The holy were always blowing themselves up, or poisoning themselves or burning their churches and temples down, or filling undergrounds with nerve gas, or getting the police to shoot them, what with it being nearly the end of the millennium.

Things didn't get much better after the millennium either.

A siege got under way. Billy Adams, a local entrepreneur, set up his hotdog stand just outside the police line and made a fine American profit feeding the police, the federal agents and the press. There were also a fair number of tangerines eaten.

Things started nicely.

The local sheriff got to use his loudspeaker which was something he really liked to do. He said things like, 'Err come on now' and 'This is silly, Stephen.'

Stephen L. Jones got to go on live TV telling everyone who would listen that he was God's messenger etc etc.

At night you could hear the little group of people huddled in the little church sing.

The church was called Riverside and it would soon be on the minds of most people on the planet for a brief while. About the time it takes for a carton of milk to go off.

You see what happened was this: there was an attempted break-out. Stephen L. Jones and his followers ran out of the great big white doors of their pretty little white church, guns a-blazing.

The police dropped their hotdogs and tangerines and fired back.

It was hell.

The twenty-six Stephen L. Jones followers surged towards the police cars parked across the drive, firing their weapons from their hips, screaming and praising the Lord.

Stephen L. Jones, bible in hand, pushed his followers on from behind.

By the time they had got halfway down the little winding drive, most were dead amid the thirty-five species of wild flowers that no one had counted.

By the time they had reached the police line, only one follower of the Ostrich Preacher was alive.

She was alive because no one would shoot at her.

Policemen just lowered their guns. The woman was armed with a Chinese assault rifle made when China was officially atheist and the largest producer of soya beans in the world. The rifle was modelled on the Soviet AK47 and had been used for a time by the IRA. It was accurate when fired in single shots but was difficult to control on automatic. The woman fired on full automatic or 'rock and roll' mode.

The reason the policemen lowered their weapons was because the woman had strapped her three babies to her body.

In the end she killed four policemen and wounded ten before Sergeant S. Gillham fired five rounds at her. Three of the rounds hit the woman, killing her instantly. The fourth bullet hit one of the babies in the head and the baby died instantly. The fifth bullet punctured another baby's lung. The wound made a sssssssssss noise as the baby's tiny right lung collapsed. That baby died in an air ambulance.

The baby who survived was Edgar Malroy.

The woman who strapped her three babies to her body was called Mary and she died following the orders of a man who claimed to be God's messenger etc etc.

Was he?
  Who knows?

China was at one point the largest producer of porcelain in the world.

PART ONE

1

I climbed Mount Everest eighty thousand years ago. I am the last supermarket trolley alive. Aloha.

I once bet £500,000 that God existed. I was a nut. Thanks to Edgar Malroy I am better now. Really.

I was made on the 3rd of November 2022, at 11.30 a.m., in an industrial estate on the outskirts of Chelmsford.

After I rolled off the production line I was greeted by a technician with a friendly face. She tapped me on my push-bar and said the first words I ever heard. Which were: 'Who's a pretty boy then?'
Which was how I discovered my sexuality.

For a time I considered the technician with the friendly face a mother of sorts.
We all did I suppose.

The technician who told me my sex and tapped me on my push-bar was called Kitty Fitzgerald. She earned £9.50 an hour in 2022. She was not incredibly enthusiastic about my existence. She said, 'Who's a pretty boy then?' casually, as if she was uninterested. In fact, she couldn't have cared less.

The reason why Kitty Fitzgerald couldn't have cared less about me or the other fifty trolleys she looked after was this: three weeks earlier she had come home to find her husband having sex with the family vacuum cleaner.
They got a divorce and she never spoke to the vacuum cleaner again.

?

This is how I climbed Mount Everest: Slowly.

2

Little Edgar Malroy was the sole survivor of the Riverside Siege. His blood-soaked little body appeared on TV and in the newspapers. He was just three weeks old at the time. Fourteen hundred families from all over the world offered to look after little Edgar. In the end he was flown back to Britain to live with his aunt and uncle.

Little Edgar's uncle was a financial planning manager for a well-known bank. Little Edgar's aunt looked after the geese, the three pigs and the six ostriches on their farm, just outside Chichester.

In 1998 ostrich meat was the single fastest-growing meat product in the Western hemisphere.

Edgar's aunt and uncle were devout agnostics.

Edgar's first words were these:
  'Who knows?'

?

Memories of what you could call my own childhood are still crystal clear, thanks to my near faultless memory system (the ZEm 12000 Nexus), which was designed, like everything else that makes up my mind, by George Milles Jr.

My very first day on Earth was spent learning to push myself around the aisles of a fake supermarket, weaving around technicians pretending to be customers. That was the sum total of my first day on Earth.

My first night was spent dreaming about supermarkets. I still dream of supermarkets all the way out here.

I have loved two women in my long and somewhat ridiculous life. One was Kitty Fitzgerald, and one was completely nuts.

?

Edgar Malroy in time grew into a bright and healthy young man.

My own childhood of sorts lasted in total three weeks. That it was so short is really not all that remarkable; some butterflies are born, grow up and die in the space of a special offer.

I was programmed with things the company, ShopALot, deemed I should know, things like the time yogurt normally took to go off, how late we stayed open until, the history of products and so on.

Such programming took place using a direct-feed interface and was an efficient way to fill my Infinity Chip with information, much more efficient than a lecture.

Although I did have one lecture, of a sort.

We had been told that shortly before we were due to leave for the real supermarkets, we would be given a few words of support and advice from the managing director of the trolley department of ShopALot.

?

This is what Graham Shipton, the managing director of the trolley department of ShopALot said to us in his lecture of sorts.

'Aloha. Are you all comfortable? Excited about your future with us at ShopALot? You know, before I came to work here I had accumulated a modest fortune in used boxes. That's right, used boxes. I recycled them. Largest recycler of used boxes, cardboard mostly, in the country. I was rolling in it. I had all the money a guy could use, but there was something missing. I didn't know what I was supposed to do. And you know what? I still don't. My entire life is spent trying to convince myself that I am doing what I am supposed to do. That I am following 'the plan', that I am fulfilling my purpose. Am I supposed to be telling you this, now? Was I supposed to shave this morning? In my office I sit there and wonder whether I ought really to be in the office across the road. Maybe I am meant to be there. Maybe that's my purpose. Maybe I'm not doing what I am supposed to do. Take my brother, he makes curtains, even makes the funny little rings. Maybe that's what I should be doing, making curtains. Let me tell you something; when I was a kid I wanted to be a dental technician more then anything else in the world, but something happened. An uncle took me for a ride in a hot-air balloon and I lost interest. I grew out of it, I guess.

'Now I just don't know. Not knowing your purpose is a terrible fate, believe me, it's a terrible thing.

'You on the other hand have been blessed with a clearly defined, easily grasped purpose. You are and always will be supermarket trolleys. 'The plan' of your entire lives is crystal clear. Your destinies are as predictable as can be and, well, I just want you to know that I envy you guys.'

Graham Shipton then told a joke. It was the first joke I ever heard.

Do you know what Edgar Malroy would have done had he heard that lecture, of a sort, by Graham Shipton, the managing director of the trolley department of ShopALot? Edgar Malroy would have dropped his trousers.

3

'There was this man who worked in a nuclear power plant and every day he would leave the plant with a wheelbarrow full of rubbish.

'The security guard at the gate became suspicious. Becoming suspicious was, after all, his job.

'One day the security guard accused the man of stealing.

'The man denied it at first but then confessed, to stealing wheelbarrows.'

Graham Shipton told us that he had a golden rule, a rule that would make our time on Earth more worthwhile.

His golden rule was this: always say to your customers when you meet them for the first time or when they leave, 'Aloha.'

He told us it was the Hawaiian word for hello and goodbye. Maybe it still is.

Mr Shipton made us say it out loud five times, then he had different trolleys do each of the sounds, then he divided us into two groups so that one group said 'Alo' and the other group said 'ha'. I was in the 'ha' group.

Then Mr Shipton looked at his watch, waved at us enthusiastically and said that he thought he was supposed to be somewhere else, although he wasn't sure, and left.

We all said 'Aloha.'

My three-week childhood of sorts came to an end after Mr Shipton's lecture. As we boarded the trucks bound for the real supermarkets, two by two, Kitty Fitzgerald gave us all a piece of advice. She told us to be careful out there.

*　　*　　*

I like to think she actually meant it.

4

I am as far as I know the only supermarket trolley in the history of the world to have a diploma. It is in agnosticism and from Who Knows College.

I brought it with me into space. I even had it framed. It's in bad shape now. It's been hit by micro-meteorites.

Most have been the size of garden peas.

?

Edgar Malroy died in the wink of an eye. It was without a doubt what millions all over the planet wanted. There were street parties in fact.

Edgar Malroy's epitaph reads:

Not sleeping but dead.

The same inscription was put on the graves of the six thousand employees of Scepticism Inc. that perished along with him.

?

Edgar Malroy always misspelt Scepticism. Whenever I pointed this out to him he would say, 'How do you know?'

?

Edgar Malroy fell in love on the 14th of January 2024. He fell in love just like that. I know. I was there.

Later he would ask me whether it was possible to disagree with someone violently, absolutely, to consider them immoral and nuts and yet still love them.

I told him I thought it was a long shot.

5

George Milles Jr, the inventor of the Infinity Chip, and the second wealthiest man ever, died nearly a year before I was made.

His coffin was unusual. It would rotate, rather like a kebab spit, so that it could be said that he was turning in his grave.

This is what it says on George Milles Jr's gravestone:

> *A taste for dirty stories may be said to be inherent in the human animal.*
>
> George Moore (1888)

He was buried on Easter Island, along with six hundred of his favourite wives. Aloha.

George Milles Jr had fourteen hundred wives. He had called them all Sarah to avoid confusion.

Each night one of his fourteen hundred wives had been sent a card inviting them to his bedroom.

There they would watch TV for a bit, eat popcorn and then make love.

?

By 2022 there were thirty-eight different brands of popcorn in any branch of ShopALot.

Aztec priests used to wear amulets of stringed popcorn in religious ceremonies. They really did.

American Indians were said to have brought bags of popcorn to the Plymouth Pilgrims for their Thanksgiving dinner in 1621.

?

Edgar Malroy used to say that the Old World should celebrate Thanksgiving too, because we had got rid of so many religious nuts when the American colonies were set up.

?

One brand of popcorn we had on sale in the supermarket in 2022 was called Popecorn and was distributed by the Vatican.

The information on the packet stated that each piece of Popecorn had been individually coated in sugar and blessed by a Bishop.

It also said on the packet that Popecorn could be eaten as a snack anywhere but was best eaten when watching one of Pope John John's many films.

In 2022, 300 million pounds of popcorn were popped world-wide.

?

George Milles Jr bought, among other things, most of the south of France.

When George Milles Jr died the stock market crashed, as a matter of course, and most of his wives changed their names.

George Milles Jr had a rather unusual funeral. It took place in the Barringer Crater, which was at the time the largest crater on Earth. It was 1.2 kilometres in diameter and had been caused by a meteorite weighing two million tons crashing into the Earth around forty thousand years ago.

George Milles Jr's body was placed in a coffin, and surrounded by fifty thousand orange plastic chairs cemented to the floor of the giant crater. The floor of the Barringer Crater was 175 metres deep.

Representatives from every country came to George Milles Jr's funeral, as did everyone with a last name beginning with E. Lots of people didn't get an orange plastic chair cemented to the floor of the giant crater to sit on.

Speeches were read out, tributes made, scores settled. Pope John John said that George Milles Jr had been a very wealthy man, with a great taste in music, and a lot of wives.

The Dalai Lama laughed so hard his false teeth fell out.

The UN Secretary General said this of George Milles Jr:

'He was like a great big blue pill. It sure as hell worked but it had pretty bad side-effects and what was the illness?'

Everyone wanted to know how George Milles Jr had invented the Infinity Chip but nobody ever found out.

Then seven hundred Alpine yodellers started to yodel like mad, and five hundred Indian elephants performed a small dance routine in the middle of the crater.

Halfway through the elephant routine, from launch silos in America and Russia, hundreds of intercontinental missiles were launched into the upper atmosphere.

Back in the crater, the elephants received a standing ovation.

This was followed by a coloured water display by the New York fire department.

After that the entire Scandinavian air force flew over the crater and dropped a total of ten thousand rubber ducks each equipped with a parachute and a tape recorder which automatically played 'Bustin Surfboards' by the Tornadoes once the ducks dropped below five thousand feet.

As the tape recorders began playing a massive radio transmission was sent out into space from the world's largest radio telescope, the Arecibo, in Puerto Rico. (Puerto Rico's main exports in 2022 were processed sugar and vacuum cleaner parts.)

The message went as follows:

I, George Milles Jr, died on 14th January 2022.
I was the wealthiest, cleverest, kindest man ever to live on this world.
I'm gone, you missed me. Your loss.
George Milles Jr died of life.
I was great!

By the time the transmission, sent out on a wavelength of twenty-one centimetres, had finished, the intercontinental missiles launched from America and Russia were seven miles above the Barringer Crater. The intercontinental missiles exploded, sending hundreds of tons of crushed garlic into the air above the crater and for months afterwards the Pacific ocean tasted a bit funny.

It really did.

A helicopter then picked up George Milles Jr's coffin from the centre of the Barringer Crater, its rotor blades cutting into the falling cloud of crushed garlic, and carried George Milles Jr's remains to Easter Island.

Two days later everyone on Earth was sent a photograph of the second wealthiest man ever.

6

We filed off the trucks two by two into our gleaming white, brand new supermarket. We were all nervous wrecks. We didn't know what to say, it was all too much for us.

Behind our store was St Pancras coroner's office and through a window we could see a fat lady putting dead people's clothes on hangers. Behind the coroner's office were row upon row of train tracks.

Next door to our supermarket was an ancient little church that would become, thanks to Edgar Malroy, the most famous little church in the world.

?

There were fourteen different soap powders in every ShopALot store. Thirteen were marketed by the Italian-based multinational L. Beno, the other brand was called 'St Martha Powder' and was marketed by the Vatican.

St Martha was the sister of Mary Magdalen, the patron saint of prostitutes. (Reformed.)

St Martha was the patron saint of housewives.

On the front of the packets of St Martha Powder was the claim that Sisters in the Vatican used St Martha Powder when they cleaned Pope John John's cassock.

Edgar Malroy used to call Pope John John, among other things, a drag queen.

?

After our initial shock we became accustomed to our supermarket; in fact in no time at all we became bored out of our Infinity Chips.

The only bit of excitement came on Sundays when the priest from the church next door would come in and warn our customers that they were 'shopping with their very souls'. The priest was always getting into heated discussions with our floor manager, who kept pointing outside while the priest kept pointing at the ceiling. They never pointed at the same thing. They never agreed.

'One day,' the priest would shout, 'just one day out of seven, is that asking too much? Is that unreasonable? God made everything – everything! – in six days, then he rested. We've got to follow his example. That's what it says in the Bible. It's critical that we spend

21

Sundays praising God, not shopping. Sundays,' he would say, 'are for souls, not tins of what have you – God, not groceries!'

He went on and on like that every Sunday. None of our shoppers seemed to pay much notice, but us supermarket trolleys were mesmerised. We had never seen anything like the priest before in our short, ridiculous lives. We crowded around him, praying out loud and so on.

He told us we had a divine mission to make shopping on Sundays as irritating as we possibly could, and of course, not knowing any better, we believed him and refused to be used on the Sabbath. Shoppers had to use baskets instead.

Sometimes the priest would read out passages from the Bible about Sodom and Gomorrah and say that most Bible scholars agreed that one of the many wickednesses of the two cities was that their shops had remained open on Sundays.

Sometimes the priest brought into the supermarket a giant crucifix on wheels that had a life-size Jesus holding two bags of shopping in his nailed hands. The bags would rotate around and around and knock things off shelves.

The priest's visits were the highlight of our week. When he stopped coming we were all utterly devastated.

Why the priest had stopped coming was simple; he had met Edgar Malroy.

?

After George Milles Jr's funeral a religious group took over the Barringer Crater. They were known as Second Comers, and spent every night sitting on the fifty thousand orange plastic chairs cemented to the floor of the crater, looking up at the sky, awaiting the second meteor which they believed would impact the Earth at exactly the same spot and would be even bigger than the first. The Second Comers believed that anyone directly under the meteor when it hit would be unharmed. They showed why this would be the case with complicated mathematics and a computer model. The Second Comers believed the impact of the second meteor would herald the arrival of God and his angels. The leader of the Second Comers thought he was God's messenger etc etc.

Every time there was a shooting star, one of the Second Comers would say, 'I thought that one was it for sure.'

?

I first met Edgar Malroy in 2024. He had just been expelled from his college. He was twenty-three and I was just two years old.

I had been taken against my will all the way to Regent's Park by children playing truant and was making my way back to the store when I thought of the priest and decided to find out what had become of him.

An old man at a bus stop across the road helped me up the steps of the church.

I would later single-handedly climb Everest.

Thirty-five species of wild flowers grew amid the grass which surrounded the church.

Edgar Malroy had altered the outside of the church in only two ways; he had removed the cross on the spire and replaced it with a great big question mark, and he had placed a wooden placard over the entrance of the church on which he had painted the following words:

> *The world is tired of metaphysical assertions.*
> Immanuel Kant, *Prolegomena*.

7

George Milles Jr had invented the Infinity Chip on the 16th of August 1998. He patented the idea and organised a secret auction in a Munich hotel. The world's most powerful companies gathered to hear about the chip and to offer as much money as they possibly could for it. For some reason, during the secret auction the only refreshment on offer was carrot juice. Pope John John used to drink a lot of carrot juice when he lived in California.

It is possible to photosynthesise if you drink sufficient amounts of carrot juice.

Pope John John, as far as I am aware, never masturbated or photosynthesised.

The global carrot crop in 2022 has been estimated to have been worth $200 million.

In the end the transnational company L. Beno made George Milles Jr the largest offer, and bought the right to market products with the Infinity Chip.

Just how much L. Beno paid no one really knows, but the sum of £100,287 billion was mentioned in the *Wall Street Journal*, and a similar figure was quoted in the *Financial Times*.

It was a ridiculous amount of money.

Thus did George Milles Jr become the second wealthiest man ever.

What was the Infinity Chip?

Consciousness. George Milles Jr had invented artificial intelligence. And no one ever found out how he did it.

The chairman of L. Beno at the time of the Infinity Chip

auction was Leonard Duncombe, who had turned his father's shoe-cleaning business into the largest transnational company in the world. Leonard Duncombe collected porcelain cats.

He had the second largest collection of porcelain cats in the western hemisphere. The largest being the George Eumorfopoulos collection housed in the British Museum.

?

When I ventured into the little church for the first time things were quiet. Edgar Malroy was sitting behind a stone table working at a computer.

'Aloha,' I said.

And this is what Edgar Malroy said, without looking up:

'There are thirty-five species of wild flowers in the grounds of this church.'

'How do you know?' I asked.

'I counted them. I'll tell you something else. See this desk, it's an altar, dates back to the seventh century. They say St Augustine used it.'

'Imagine that,' I said.

'Imagine that,' Edgar said.

Then I asked him where the priest was.

'Oh, he ran out of money, the poor nut,' Edgar said, and then for the first time looked up. He stared at me then said, 'Shouldn't you be next door?'

I said that he was probably right.

He smiled and then, after a little while, asked me what I believed in.

8

Leonard Duncombe bought the right to mass-produce the Infinity Chip in the same month in which his son Thomas Duncombe became an International Bible Student or a Millennial Dawnist. That is to say a Jehovah's Witness.

The Duncombes lived in Venice, in the Palazzo Corner-Contarini Dei Caralli. It had been the family's home for as long as anyone could remember. (The origins of their unItalian-sounding name was a complete mystery.) The eccentricity of the Duncombe family was legendary. It was said that they ironed all their newspapers before reading them and never used the same bar of soap twice.

What happened was this:
Thomas Duncombe got his hand stuck in the soft drink vending machine by the main entrance of his home, and two Jehovah's Witnesses swam by and freed him.

Jehovah's Witnesses believe among other things that Jesus died on a stake not a cross. They also don't celebrate Christmas.

Thomas Duncombe was put in charge of the Infinity Chip programme by his father. The plan was to install Infinity Chips in every sort of electrical appliance imaginable.

Jehovah's Witnesses don't believe in hell.
They do believe that Satan rules the world and that the show will be ending shortly.

Here is something else Jehovah's Witnesses believe:
Only 144,000 true believers will go to heaven. 144,000 out of the whole of human history.

That works out at about one person every five years.

One of those 144,000 is bound to be Charles Taze Russell, the owner of a chain of clothes stores, even though he got divorced. Once.

You see, Charles Taze Russell was the founder of the Jehovah's Witnesses. In 1909 the movement established its headquarters in New York, just around the corner from where the very first supermarket was to be opened in 1930 by a group of merchants as a means of combating chain-store competition.

In 1911 Charles Taze Russell started to wear women's clothes. 'It brings me closer to God,' he explained on innumerable occasions.

In 1913 Charles Taze Russell's wife divorced him. It had nothing to do with vacuum cleaners. In fact they were only just available at the time and were huge, the size of modern fridges, and took two people to use.

Anyway, in 1913 Charles Taze Russell got divorced and went to heaven, the first person to do so in five years. Aloha.

Two months after Charles Taze Russell got divorced and went to live in heaven Joseph Franklin Rutherford was elected president of the Jehovah's Witnesses. Joseph Franklin Rutherford unfurled a massive scroll during the Witness 1922 convention at a place called Cedar Point. On the scroll were the following words:

Advertise! Advertise! For God's sake Advertise!

Joseph Franklin Rutherford took up residence in a mansion in San Diego built by the Jehovah's Witnesses to house Abraham and the prophets upon their return to earth.

The mansion had central heating, a swimming pool (so Jesus could go running), tennis courts and a model railway in the attic which Joseph played with insensately. He said it brought him closer to God. Joseph named the little model town the trains travelled through, Bethlehem. The model town of Bethlehem had an abortion clinic and a blood transfusion clinic outside of which were tiny little model Jehovah's Witnesses in silent protest. The mansion also had five vacuum cleaners the size of fridges.

Joseph Franklin Rutherford slept in the Noah suite.

In 1997 the mansion burned down. Faulty wiring and Satan were blamed. As a matter of course. In fact fire fighters thought the whole thing had started when a light bulb, intended to be the Star of Bethlehem, had fallen onto the manger on the outskirts of the model town near the miniature plutonium dump.

The Jehovah's Witnesses started building a new mansion which would have its very own golf course. They also bought a beach house in Barbados for the prophets. It had cable TV and a helicopter landing pad.

Joseph eventually went to heaven and the Jehovah's Witnesses did away with presidents, although they still believed even in 2022 that only 144,000 people would go to heaven. In 2024 Jehovah's Witnesses would go back to electing presidents.

Work on the second mansion had only just started when Thomas Duncombe was told the Truth, had his hand freed and become a Witness.

?

Thomas Duncombe ordered that the doctrines of his particular religion be added to the Infinity Chip. This was duly done.

Early prototypes behaved awkwardly. They did not inter-act well with humans. They were obstinate and opinionated. They had nothing to say that did not refer back to scrip-ture.

They were deemed anti-social and terrible bores.

'Perfect,' said Thomas Duncombe.

'Shit,' said Leonard Duncombe when he read reports of the early prototypes. He flew to the research station in person to see what was going wrong.

Thomas asked his father when he arrived if he was happy with the way the world was.

Leonard Duncombe was so angry when he heard that his son had become a nut, and saw what he had done to the Infinity Chip, that he broke one of his porcelain cats. He always carried a porcelain cat in his hand, you see.

'It was how I met my wife,' he would explain on innumerable occasions.

Like most collectors of porcelain cats, Leonard Duncombe was a raving atheist.

Leonard Duncombe ordered all the nutty material removed from the Infinity Chip at once.

Technicians deleted all the nutty material. Nearly.

A tiny weeny little thing got overlooked.

The tiny weeny little thing that got overlooked was this: The belief in God.

Mass production began soon after that. All kinds of things were given Infinity Chips: TVs, toasters, irons, kettles, alarm clocks, dishwashers, shavers, food mixers, vacuum cleaners, even supermarket trolleys.

Conscious electrical appliances became all the rage and the old unconscious appliances were thrown out.

When no one was looking, Thomas Duncombe stole the early anti-social prototypes and handed them over to his fellow Jehovah's Witnesses. It was from these prototypes that the Ding Dong 7s were created.

?

I told Edgar Malroy that I believed in the scientific method, the laws of gravity and commerce, that man is ultimately a positive rather than a negative force in the universe, that any product with the word 'new' on its packaging really was new. I told him I believed in coupons, bulk buying, special offers and God.

9

Edgar Malroy said, 'A supermarket trolley that believes in God,' and then burst out laughing.

He laughed like this:

Ahhh-ooo Ahhh-ooo

I told him I wasn't the only one.

Then I told Edgar a joke. It was the very first joke I had heard.

After I had told the joke Edgar asked me why it was funny.

I tried to explain why it was funny. I said it was funny because you didn't expect the thing that the man was stealing to be the wheelbarrows and because it was the wheelbarrows that the man was stealing, it was funny. Put another way, the joke was funny because . . .

Eventually I gave up trying to explain the joke.

I said that it was just funny.

'And at that moment I accepted you into the crazy sad community of persons,' Edgar Malroy would say afterwards.

?

'How much do you want to bet?' Edgar Malroy asked.

'On what?'

'That God exists.'

'Huh?'

'You believe in God. Well, how much?'

'Money?'

'What else is there?'

'I don't know, how much is he worth?'

'You tell me.'

'I suppose he is worth quite a bit?'

'So how much will you give me?'

'I don't have any money.'

'You don't?'

'Not a penny.'

Edgar seemed disappointed.

'I don't normally do this, you understand,' he said, 'but you can write me an IOU if you like. Now, how much? If you don't want to bet you can't really believe.'

'Ten pounds?'

Edgar Malroy laughed.

He laughed like this:

Ahhh-ooo Ahhh-ooo

'The other day an old lady came in here and bet ten times that amount that God had existed for at least five minutes. I've got her bet somewhere here. This morning a man came in and bet sixty pounds that God was good.' Edgar Malroy thought for a moment then added, 'I get a lot of those.'

'So what happens then, after someone has made a bet?'

'Not much really. They get a badge and a receipt.'

'You mean you just keep the money?'

'Yep.'

'So why do they do it?'

'Because they're all nuts. Now how much will you give me for God's existence?'

10

'You want to bet on dull mundane things like the horses you go to a normal betting shop. You want to bet on something metaphysical you come here. By metaphysical, I mean anything that refers to absolute reality, anything which cannot be proven true or false by the senses, anything religious.'

'But how can anyone win?'

'They can't. No one ever wins. That's the point, that's the beauty of the system.'

'Suppose you wanted to bet that the Absolute enters into itself. Now I don't know for a moment what that means but I'll write the words down and I'll take your money off you if you believe it.'

'I don't get it.'

'Why does someone come in here, slap money on the table, and bet that the Holy Trinity is true? Because he is a nut.'

'But why do you take his money?'

'Isn't it obvious? To make him realise he is a nut. To show him just how irrational he is, believing in things that cannot be known. I'm in the business of showing the absurdity of all metaphysical utterances. Now how much will you give me for God?'

I gave Edgar £500,000, or rather he wrote out for me an IOU for that amount.

He never forgot or forgave. Years later he'd bring up the matter at the most inappropriate times.

I never lived it down.

Edgar Malroy fell helplessly in love sixty seconds after I bet £500,000 that God existed.

Edgar was the closest friend I ever had on Earth.

11

The exact number of Ding Dong 7s produced in secret factories in the deserts of Syria by Jehovah's Witnesses was never known, although estimates range from twenty-five thousand to thirty thousand. They were moved by train from Au Raggah along the Euphrates river to the port of Latakia and from there shipped all over the world during 2022, along with 10,000 tons of dried apricots, 60,000 tons of raisins, 4,000 tons of pistachios and 8,000 tons of shelled almonds.

The Ding Dong 7s were designed to act like humans in every way with two large exceptions; they couldn't smile and couldn't bend their legs.

?

Almonds and pistachios, Edgar Malroy told me once, were the only nuts to be mentioned in the Bible. I told him this was perfectly possible because the pistachio originated from Persia and Syria and the almond was the oldest, most widely cultivated and extensively used nut in the world.

We talked about food often.

?

Ding Dong 7s couldn't bend their legs.

They couldn't walk in fact.

?

Many years later, during the final stages of the Holy War,

Edgar Malroy told me how his metaphysical betting business had begun.

He had just been kicked out of Tewkesbury University, had absolutely no money and ended up just wandering about London eating food out of dustbins and things. Then, one Sunday, he passed a church on Pancras Road. Why he went in he couldn't remember; perhaps it was to take a piss. Anyway Edgar Malroy went in and ended up sitting at the back. There were thirty people there. A good turn-out for those days. The priest was shouting gently about the Son of God having risen from the dead. Quite without thinking Edgar raised his hand and asked a question. He said, 'How much?' Everyone turned around. The priest was so flustered he read out the same part of his sermon again. When he got to the bit about the Son of God being raised from the dead, Edgar asked his question again. 'How much?' Everyone turned round again.

The priest shook violently for a moment, looked at the floor of the pulpit then looked Edgar straight in the eye.

'W-what do you mean?'

'You believe that the Son of God rose from the dead?' Edgar said.

'Yes,' said the priest, pushing his glasses up his nose.

'Well, all I'm asking is this: how much? How much are you willing to bet that this is so?' Edgar asked.

The priest sank down into his pulpit. He looked to his left and seemed to be about to speak, then stopped himself. Three times he seemed about to speak but held back at the last minute. The congregation kept turning from the priest in the pulpit to Edgar in the back row.

The priest sank lower and lower into his pulpit until he was almost out of sight. He turned to face the altar. He prayed.

Then the priest stepped from his pulpit, walked down the aisle, ignoring the stares of his congregation, and began fiddling around in a pocket of his robe. When he reached the back row of pews the priest took out his wallet and gave Edgar Malroy £85.50 in cash.

'It's all I've got on me at the moment,' he said defensively.

The priest then pushed his glasses up his nose again and walked briskly back to his pulpit, clearing his throat a few times as he did so. He began his sermon again but no one was listening. His congregation was queuing up in the aisle to show Edgar Malroy how much they believed their funny little God guy had risen from the dead.

Later, when the collection plates were brought out, no one in the church had any money left.

What happened that first Sunday was repeated every week. It became, Edgar admitted, something of a ritual. The priest felt obliged always to give Edgar more money than anyone else, the poor nut.

This had been going on for about a month when a bishop appeared at the service one Sunday morning. Edgar was sure that the bishop was going to ask him to leave but instead he wrote out a cheque for £1,000, shook Edgar's hand and enthusiastically thanked him for allowing him to demonstrate his faith in such an open and candid manner. 'You must be from America,' he said, smiling.
   'Sort of,' Edgar said.
   'I'm refreshed,' said the bishop.
   'And I'm richer,' Edgar replied.

After that Edgar began to make serious money. More money than he knew what to do with. Three months after walking into that church for the first time, Edgar Malroy bought it and turned it into the first Metaphysical Betting Shop.

The priest and the congregation kept on turning up every Sunday until they ran out of money, as if nothing much had changed and nothing much had. The church was merely under new management.

12

Ding Dong 7s got about with the help of tiny electric wheels in the soles of their shoes.

Climbing stairs was a real problem for Ding Dong 7s. The only way they could manage stairs was to fall over and then crawl up the stairs using their hands.

?

Edgar Malroy, sixty seconds after I had made my one and only metaphysical bet, fell in love with Sophia Alderson. It was easily done. It was the easiest thing in the world, in fact.

She was so beautiful it was downright dangerous. Men would willingly die for her ears alone.

Sophia Alderson, in addition to being ridiculously beautiful, claimed to be God's messenger etc etc.

Sophia Alderson claimed to be divinely inspired by the Virgin Mother at least three times a day.
She claimed that these inspirations would come normally around eight thirty, two twenty-five and nine o'clock.

Sophia Alderson claimed to have seen the Virgin on at least forty-five occasions. She claimed in fact that they were the very closest of friends.

Sophia Alderson had a wall chart in her bedsit on which a green mark meant an inspiration and a blue mark meant a visitation.

Sophia Alderson had a red marker which she was saving for the end of the world.

Sophia Alderson was a very sizeable nut indeed.
She was also, like I said, ridiculously beautiful.

?

This is what happened:
Edgar had just written out my IOU when Sophia walked into the church shouting about the end of the world. She was wearing a sandwich board which had written on it in blue biro the following message:

ALL PEOPLE MUST REPENT
AND STOP DOING EVIL
OR THEY SHALL BE CAST
INTO HELL-FIRE
DAMNATION
TORMENT AND PAIN
FOREVER

Edgar looked at her. He looked at her for quite some time.

Later he would say that seeing Sophia for the first time was like finding an Easter egg on a sunny afternoon by a lake in the middle of September.

I don't think Edgar read Sophia's sandwich board, that seemed to interest him least of all. He looked at her face and then he looked at her hands and then he looked at her legs. When Edgar looked at Sophia's legs he started to mumble about the infinite.
That was the only time I ever heard Edgar Malroy mumble about the infinite.

Sophia stopped ranting on about the end of the world and looked at Edgar.
'Hello,' she said.

'Hi,' said Edgar.

Then Sophia turned to me. 'Shouldn't you be next door?' she said.

I said she was probably right.

Sophia asked Edgar where the priest was.

'He ran out of money about a week ago,' Edgar said.

'Who took down the cross?' Sophia asked, pointing beautifully at the ceiling.

'I did,' smiled Edgar.

'Why?'

Edgar put his arm on Sophia's perfect shoulder and whispered into her porcelain-like ear the idea behind the Metaphysical Betting Shop.

When the Metaphysical Betting Shop had been explained to her, Sophia Alderson prayed.

After a little while Sophia ceased praying and said that God wanted the whole thing stopped before it all got out of hand.

Sophia Alderson and Edgar Malroy argued after that for twelve hours non-stop. They argued like billy-o.

I thought it wise to leave when they started really shouting at each other. Sophia helped me down the steps, screaming at Edgar, who was standing in the entrance to the church, calling Sophia all kinds of things.

He called her a demented nut, a community care case, a silly little girl who had never grown up, a person with a comic case of egotism, a superstitious old cow, and an irrational bitch.

For her part Sophia called Edgar Malroy a smartarse, a smug little intellectual nitwit, a pagan, a sinner, an abomination, a spawn of Satan, and a creature from the deepest pit of hell. Sophia Alderson didn't swear. To swear meant you went to hell. Lots of things meant you went to hell, including: picking one's nose, wearing odd socks, using a condom, eating toast, looking at naked animals, reading in bed, telling knock-knock jokes, playing ball games on Sunday, using a microwave on Sunday, breaking wind, smoking, worshipping idols, drinking anything other than carrot juice, eating with your fingers, indecency, not saying grace, listening to non-religious music, going to a co-ed school, not praying fifty times a day, enjoying sex, watching immodesty on television, slovenliness, leaving the washing-up for more than three days, watching two videos in a row, and so on.

13

Edgar Malroy and Sophia Alderson's lengthy and heated argument that afternoon was interrupted by a number of nuts who came into the betting shop: a Buddhist who wanted to place a £20 bet that Buddhist meditation will produce the conditions that allow a person to see absolute reality; a Muslim who wanted to make a £85 bet that the Angel Gabriel brought the revelation of the Qur'an to Mohammed; a realist who wanted to bet £100 that whatever exists has its character independent of it being perceived by man or God; a West African witch doctor who bet £30 that Nzambi is the creator and master of the world, and has gone away because of man's crimes against him; an unemployed Pythagorean who wanted to bet £50 that numbers hold the key to the absolute; a Thevsrada Buddhist from Edinburgh who bet £52 that everything is impermanent and in flux, then changed the bet to £20 when he realised he wouldn't have enough money for the train fare home; a member of the Order of the Lunar Temple who bet £250 that he and his spiritual brothers were reincarnations of medieval knights who would soon journey through fire to the planet Sirius, where God lives in another dimension, on Tuesdays; a Marcoin Gnostic undergoing therapy who bet £3 that Simon Magus was the first and supreme God; a Christian who bet £500 that a convicted criminal had been raised by God from the dead and was the Messiah for whom Israel had been waiting; and an old lady with four bags of shopping who bet £17.32 that David Icke had been God's messenger etc etc.

I know because I have downloaded into my ZEm 12000 Nexus all the metaphysical bets that Edgar Malroy ever took.

?

At seven Edgar closed the Metaphysical Betting Shop. He and Sophia continued to argue sitting on the grass outside amid the thirty-five species of counted wild flowers.

Because of her sandwich board Sophia looked very uncomfortable sitting on the grass outside the Metaphysical Betting Shop amid the thirty-five species of counted wild flowers. She absolutely refused to take it off though.

A funny thing happened when Edgar Malroy and Sophia Alderson argued on the grass outside the Metaphysical Betting Shop, amid the thirty-five species of counted wild flowers. Sophia was telling Edgar that the whole universe was built to a most wondrous plan, that everything that happened, happened with a purpose, when a pigeon shat on Sophia's golden hair.

Edgar Malroy was sceptical about the purpose people had in saying there was a purpose to life. Whenever anyone talked about purpose, and a lot of religious nuts did, Edgar Malroy would drop his trousers.

Which is what he did outside the Metaphysical Betting Shop as Sophia Alderson tried to remove part of God's wondrous plan from her beautiful golden hair.

?

Once Ding Dong 7s had been operational for a few weeks the number of people becoming Jehovah's Witnesses around the world jumped tenfold.

Thomas Duncombe was made President of the Jehovah's Witnesses. He didn't know what to say. He took up golf and got a

40

mouth ulcer. Thomas Duncombe thought that his mouth ulcer brought him closer to Jesus Christ.

When he heard of the election, Thomas Duncombe's father publicly disowned his son.

As if to make matters worse between himself and his father, Thomas Duncombe flew to London the day after Edgar and Sophia met and placed a bet at the Metaphysical Betting Shop. The very first major religious leader to do so.

Edgar called Thomas Duncombe a nut and gave him his receipt and badge. Thomas Duncombe said he would always wear the badge with pride and asked Edgar if he would like to buy a copy of the *Watchtower* magazine. Edgar called the President of the Jehovah's Witnesses a nut, again.

Thomas Duncombe, like myself, had bet £500,000 that God existed.

14

'Chuck' Chisholme, who later became Pope John John, was born in Santa Barbara, California, in 1965. Claims that he was a member of the street gang 'White Snakes' have never been adequately proven.

California produced for most of the twentieth and early twenty-first centuries more almonds than all the other places in the world put together.

The future Pope, while watching the TV programme *Wheel of Fortune* at the age of five, inserted a frozen garden pea in his left ear which was not removed until 2021 when his mother, by then ninety-four, remembered it was still in there.

The almond crop of California is not based on the seeds planted by

Christian missionaries brought from Spain (the largest producer of tomatoes in Europe in 2022). No, the almond crop of California comes from trees brought from the East in 1843.

The year of the great potato famine in Ireland.

At the age of just sixteen Chuck dropped out of school and moved to Los Angeles, where he became a carpet cleaner. Much has been made by journalists and scholars of the metaphorical significance of this profession. As the young Chuck cleaned mankind's carpets, so he would later remove stains from their very hearts.

Just as Jesus had been a carpenter.

?

Edgar once asked me why it was that the supposed son of God spent most of his life making chairs.

'Who knows?' I said.

?

Many of the houses that the Pope cleaned in the 1980s and 90s were upon his pontification turned into shrines. The residents of 16 Trigger Street reported to the media in 2020 that the face of Jesus H. Christ was discernible on the carpet in their spare bedroom. Overnight the house was besieged by Catholics.

The Coombs, residents of 16 Trigger Street, made a fine American profit charging a compulsory voluntary contribution for upkeep of the spare bedroom.

They also made thousands when marketing men from the Vatican filmed a series of commercials for a carpet cleaner product in their spare bedroom.

The carpet cleaner was called Cardinal Cleaner and had the very latest electronic technology installed in it so that every time the carton was shaken a short benediction would follow.

Cardinal Cleaner was one of the products in the St Martha, patron saint of housewives, range.

The first thing many Californians heard of the 2021 earthquake was their Cardinal Cleaners mumbling in Latin under their kitchen sinks.

15

The reason Edgar Malroy would drop his trousers whenever he heard someone mention life having a purpose was because just after leaving Tewkesbury University he had a piece of text tattooed on his left buttock.

?

In 2023 the first of what would turn out to be a series of unusual murders took place.

A Mr Martin, a one-legged retired financial planning manager with cancer, was found by his milkman on his doorstep beaten to death.

Over the days and weeks that followed a number of similar murders were investigated by police forces all over the world.

All the murders seemed random and apparently motiveless, for no money, groceries or valuables were ever taken. People were just found dead on their doorsteps, as if they had been beaten about the body with an object such as a book.

Police forces were baffled; the only clue was this: each victim was found clutching a copy of the *Watchtower* magazine.

?

Edgar Malroy showed Sophia Alderson the text he had had

tattooed on his left buttock and they did not speak for two months.

?

Then one fine morning Sophia Alderson arrived outside the Metaphysical Betting Shop wearing her sandwich board and holding the hand of a tiny Catholic priest. She looked even more beautiful than she had done before, Edgar insisted, when he recounted the whole thing over and over to me years later. The tiny priest started sprinkling holy water from a watering can over the thirty-five species of wild flowers that grew in the grass around the church and Sophia unfurled a massive scroll she had obviously made herself. On the scroll were the following words:

Betting is sinning.

Edgar Malroy, who had just taken a £3,000 bet made by an Asceticist from Dagenham that denial of sensual gratification is a means of achieving spiritual awareness, a £68 bet from a Hindu that the Vedas contain all true knowledge, and a £48 bet from a former convict that God knows all of man's deeds and thoughts, ran out of the Metaphysical Betting Shop and demanded that the priest make a bet or leave. When the priest refused to place a bet Edgar threatened him with a giant question mark, which he kept by the door of the Metaphysical Betting Shop for just such occasions. At this point Sophia Alderson swore she saw the Virgin Mary ride by on a penny-farthing blowing bubbles.

Edgar Malroy asked for Sophia to leave immediately and for her to give him her telephone number. She did both.

She did both because the Virgin Mary she had just seen ride by on a penny-farthing blowing bubbles held precariously a sign which said:

Leave Immediately and Give Edgar Malroy
Your Telephone Number.

?

The tiny priest with the watering can loved Sophia Alderson more than anything else in the world. He had fallen in love with her years before when she had driven him from Richmond Road to Chiswick in a taxi cab. She had told him the end of the world was coming. He had told her she had lovely ears. Then when they were nearing Chiswick, he told her he would do anything for her. She said become a priest.

He tipped her and said that he would.

Sophia Alderson was ridiculously beautiful.

?

By the time all the Ding Dong 7s were rounded up, quoting scripture wildly and lashing out with their blood-soaked bibles, 12,720 people had been murdered on their doorsteps, four times that number had narrowly escaped death and nearly one million more people had become Jehovah's Witnesses.

16

The Jehovah's Witnesses High Council gave a press conference at which they expressed their deepest regret at the killings. They gave a sincere promise not to bother in the future any of the relations of the victims of the Ding Dong 7s.

It was a nice thought.

Even so, many thousands left the Church, Kingdom Halls were firebombed and in France and Canada the religion or cult was banned altogether.

The newly completed second mansion, intended to house the prophets when they returned to Earth, was blown sky high by Anti-Jehovah's Witnesses activists known as Jehovah's Witnesses Witnesses.

The few Jehovah's Witnesses that remained decided not to bother building a third mansion, agreeing instead to put the prophets up in hotels when they returned to Earth.

Thomas Duncombe, the President of the Jehovah's Witnesses and the man responsible for the Ding Dong 7 horror, disappeared.

Just before he disappeared he phoned a radio station and said that his faith remained unshaken.

?

This is the piece of text that Edgar Malroy had tattooed on his left buttock which he would show people whenever they talked about the purpose of life:

> 'What alone can our teaching be? That no one gives a human being his qualities: not God, not society, not his parents or ancestors, not he himself ... No one is accountable for existing at all, or for being constituted as he is, or for living in the circumstances and surroundings in which he lives ... He is not the result of special design, a will, a purpose; he is not the subject of an attempt to attain to an 'ideal of man' or an 'ideal happiness' or an 'ideal of morality' – it is absurd to want to hand over his nature to some purpose or other. We invented the concept 'purpose': in reality purpose is lacking.'
>
> Friedrich Nietzsche, The Twilight of the Idols, p.54

17

Edgar Malroy and Sophia Alderson started to argue on the phone every night. Sophia Alderson told Edgar that he had to stop his evil enterprise.

Edgar Malroy said, 'Ditto.'

Then Edgar would shout down the phone that one should believe something only in accordance with the evidence for it and Sophia would smash plates in frustration and partly for the sound effect in her bedsit each time Edgar stubbornly refused to accept the premise of a living God.

?

Chuck Chisholme began cleaning six carpets a day.

He also discovered his life-long passions: surfing and bungee-jumping.

Surfing was Chuck's real passion.

It was while Chuck was surfing that he came into contact with the Calvary Chapel's Radical Street Ministry, an Evangelical body intent on bringing sinners to the love of Jesus.

At first Chuck was hostile. 'I think the first words I said to these Jesus freaks, as they were known then, was fuck off.'

When the future head of the Universal Church, the vicar of Christ, St Peter's successor, God's messenger etc etc was asked by a Jesus freak back in 1996 if he believed in God, Chuck Chisholme was silent for a moment, then said this: 'Don't be stupid.'

?

Edgar Malroy and Sophia Alderson sent each other essays which they would cover in copious notes, queries and counter arguments and send back.

No no no no no! Sophia Alderson would write on Edgar's essays that had titles like 'The Virtue of Reason' or 'Why Religions Are Like Cereals' or 'Who Knows?'

Edgar would write Nuts! Nuts! Nuts! at the end of Sophia's essays, which always included elaborate pictures of shrines and saints, and had names like 'The Absolute Certainty of God's Existence' or 'God That He Exists' or 'Toast: Why it is Wrong' or 'The End Of The World' or 'Why Edgar Malroy Will Burn In Hell For Ever And Ever'.

18

This is principally why Edgar Malroy had been expelled from Tewskesbury University: He wrote a letter to the Dean.

Edgar Malroy's letter to the Dean went like this:

Dear Dean,
I am writing in accordance with section 9 of the Joining Instructions for the Autumn Term 2020, concerning religious beliefs.
I am, you see, a Winbo. We are not a very large religion; in fact as far as I am aware I am the only Winbo in your country at present.
My religion insists that I pray to God, the real and true God, often.
Every three minutes in fact.
This is the central tenet of my faith and I lose much sleep because of it.
I assure you that my praying, which involves running on the spot, will not disrupt classes. If my teachers agree I will perform my praying in a corner of the classroom or if they would prefer I could always pray in the hallway.
There are also a number of days in any year when I must refrain from doing anything, except from holding my nose, which has deep

symbolic meaning in my religion. These days, known as Winbo days, occur on the 1st, 2nd, 3rd, 4th, 5th, 8th, 14th, and 21st of each month. Obviously I will be unable to attend classes or do any kind of work on such days.

I trust my religious beliefs can be accommodated with the needs of university life.

My father was a Winbo and his father before him and his before him. I don't know what my great great grandfather believed but he was probably a Winbo too.

I must now pray.

May you come to see the true light.

Yours sincerely,

Edgar Malroy.

?

In May 1996 Activists from Calvary Chapel's Radical Street Ministry, acting on orders from the Pastor John Britain, began taking surfers' towels left unattended on the beach and leaving a small note informing the owners that the missing towels could be collected at 11.30 from the Calvary Chapel.

So a bunch of very irate surfers marched up to the chapel, including the future Pope, dripping wet.

Inside the chapel Chuck Chisholme found compassion, love, the living God Jesus H. Christ and his towel.

It was a very moving time.

19

Sophia and Edgar started to go out to argue. They would go to a restaurant, pausing in their argument only to order. When the food came Sophia would pray to God in thanks and Edgar would tut. It became something of a ritual.

Sophia prayed beautifully.

Sophia also always drank carrot juice. Though, like the Pope, she neither photosynthesised nor masturbated as far as I know.

How beautiful was Sophia Alderson? She was as beautiful as the stagnant pool out of which life arose.

She was as beautiful as the Tarantula Nebula seen in infra-red.

She was as beautiful as all of George Milles Jr's wives put together.

She was as beautiful as beautiful can be.

?

Chuck Chisholme became a central figure in the Calvary Chapel's Radical Street Ministry. Like the other Jesus Freaks Chuck would knock on strangers' doors and tell them about Jesus and hug them. In addition Chuck would often examine their carpets and suggest cleaning agents.

Then in 1998 Italian racing car magnate Enzo Ferrari's half cousin died and Chuck became a Catholic.

?

Four days later young Edgar had received a letter from the Dean. It went like this:

> *Mr Malroy,*
> *I would be grateful if you will come in to see me as soon as possible.*
> *Yours,*
>
> *Dr Matthews*
> *The Dean*

20

Edgar Malroy's essay 'Why Religions Are Like Cereals', written for Sophia Alderson, served as the basis of my dissertation for my diploma in agnosticism. It argued that Christianity is broadly like cornflakes, traditional, out of touch and falling in sales; Catholicism is cornflakes with added sugar; Protestantism comes in those individual packets; and Evangelical Christianity is just more expensive.

(In a footnote Edgar Malroy suggested that the David Koresh Waco sect was like one of those individual cornflakes you find which has been over-cooked.)

Judaism is like All Bran, dull. Islam is like bran flakes, sharing a lot of heritage with Judaism and Christianity but being a little harder to swallow. Hinduism is like muesli, which looks different but it too in time becomes boring. Buddhism is like porridge, again somewhat different to the others but there is not a whole lot in it.

New Age religions, argued Edgar Malroy, are like Fruit and Fibre, because of their many ingredients. Raisins: palm reading; hazelnuts: tarot cards; dried coconut: horoscopes; currants: pyramid power; bananas: crystal power; and apples: numerology etc etc.

Another thing Edgar Malroy argued in 'Why Religions Are Like Cereals' was that all religions are essentially the same.

Edgar Malroy said in 'Why Religions Are Like Cereals' that he preferred toast.

'Why Religions Are Like Cereals' ended with a quote by Charlotte Gilman. It went like this: *To swallow and follow, whether old doctrine or new, is a weakness still dominating the human mind.*

Sophia Alderson wrote No no no no no! on her copy of 'Why

Religions Are Like Cereals' and sent it back. Even Sophia's
scribbles were beautiful.

?

Chuck Chisholme was ordained a priest on the 12th of September
1998. In 2001 he was sent by Archbishop Griffin to take a
doctorate at the Anglican College in Rome. Chuck's dissertation
compared St Antony's (the patron saint of skin rashes) mystical
experiences with those of Neil Booker, the then world surf
champion, and received the lowest marks possible.

Undeterred, the future Pope returned to California and set up
his KoolAid Ministry, a simple hut on the beach from where he
refreshed the bodies of the public with KoolAid and their minds
with the word of God. Both for free.

Most of Chuck's work though was done on the waves themselves. He offered spiritual support for surfing souls all over the
West Coast. He even married a couple half a mile off Long Beach
on an incredible swell ten to fifteen feet high.

?

Three months before Sophia Alderson was born her mother
announced to friends and family that God had impregnated her,
told her she was not like the other girls he had been with and that
she would have a son who would be the Messiah and would never use
a phone book in his life. He would be born on the 16th of September.
He would have brown eyes and in later years develop a bald patch,
live in cheap motel rooms and never take no for an answer.

Sophia was born on the 5th of September in Warsaw in 1996
and had brilliant blue eyes like her father who was a violinist in
the Polish National Orchestra.

Sophia's sex caused problems in her relationship with her
mother, and her mother's relationship with God. In fact Sophia's
mother and God never spoke again. There was not even a card
at Christmas.

In 1999 the directors of the Polish National Orchestra realised that Sophia's father couldn't play the violin and had never, in his thirty years in the orchestra, played a note. He had simply moved the bow over the top of the strings.

The only noise he had ever made, in fact, was the occasional cough or when he moved his chair.

The family moved abruptly to England, where Sophia's father became a disc jockey. In England Sophia became very religious after the swing in the back garden broke. She wrote off to all the major religions and browsed through their colour catalogues picking in the end Christianity. She slept with her arms out wide and was, like so many Polish girls with musically failed fathers forced to live in England, determined to become a saint. She began to wear only white underwear. She became so religious that she would say 'thee' instead of 'you'.

It was during this time that Sophia had her first vision. She saw the Virgin Mother skate though the living room clutching a sign which said:

Don't Eat Meat.

So she didn't.

She allowed God and the Holy Spirit to guide her through her exams.

She failed everything including woodwork.

Her teachers loved her anyway.

When Sophia's father was found to have simply tuned into another radio station and broadcast that, her family had to flee again. Sophia decided to stay in London, partly because the Virgin Mother appeared one night wearing rock-climbing equipment on the wall of her room with a sign that said:

Stay in London.

Sophia Alderson was twenty-two at the time and more beautiful than a supermarket trolley with a diploma in agnosticism can put into words.

?

Chuck Chisholme had a special surfboard made. It had a cross on one side and a life-size picture of the Virgin Mary on the other.

In 2003 Chuck founded the Surfers for Christ, who used crucifix-shaped surfboards and competed in national and international surfboard contests. The Surfers for Christ never won anything because of the shape of their surfboards.

Eventually the group disbanded, possibly because of pressure put on two of the group by Jehovah's Witnesses who believed, among other things, that Jesus died on a stake not a cross.

When Chuck became Pope in 2021 one of the first things he did was to initiate the lengthy procedure of canonising world surf champion Neil Brooker.

Neil Brooker was beatified in 2023 and a few years later there were over forty-five shrines to him all along the West Coast.

?

Edgar went to see the Dean as soon as possible.

The Dean invited Edgar into his office. The Dean asked Edgar to sit down. Which he did. The Dean then handed Edgar the letter he had written about Winboism. The Dean asked Edgar to explain the letter.

Edgar said that it had been a joke.

The Dean then asked Edgar to stand up. Edgar stood up. Then the Dean told Edgar that he never wanted to see him again. Ever.

Edgar told the Dean he thought he was being unreasonable.

Things got heated after that. Edgar was thrown out of the Dean's office.

?

Chuck Chisholme directed his first film after becoming a cardinal in 2010. It was called 'Saul and the Seer'. Chuck Chisholme would be killed during the great Mania when a Vatican electric tin-opener removed the top half of his cranium.

It would be the most horrific way in which a Pope had gone to heaven.

?

Edgar Malroy should have written a nice grovelly letter to the Dean.

But he didn't. He had a problem with authority.

What he did was this: he had a meeting with the students' union and a week later an article appeared in the campus paper condemning the university for religious intolerance.

And yes, Edgar Malroy got up during his first class and ran on the spot every three minutes amid laughter and demands for him to sit down.

?

The second time I saw Edgar Malroy he was shot by a 75mm recoilless cannon.

21

The canteen buzzed with the issue of whether it was permissible to run on the spot every three minutes for religious reasons in class and within no time at all the University of Tewkesbury divided into Winbo supporters and anti-Winbos.

?

Sophia Alderson moved into a bedsit in South London after her parents left the country.

She was so holy she never made any friends.

Men fell helplessly in love with her of course. Normally about three a day. Sophia was only interested in Jesus Christ. All the men who fell in love with Sophia ended up Christian.

In fact the only man who fell hopelessly in love with Sophia Alderson and did not become a Christian was Edgar Malroy.

Sophia Alderson was so holy that she found it very hard to keep jobs. She was always breaking down in joy at God's Love, underlining passages from the Bible or praying.

Despite this Sophia somehow managed to get enough money to visit Lourdes, where she became very ill, along with around three thousand other pilgrims.

While recovering in hospital she had her third vision. The Virgin Mother in a hot air balloon tapped on the window of the hospital.

Sophia believed that the Holy Mother was trying to send her a message.

Sophia never found out what the message was, though she thought it might have something to do with the structure of a carbon-dioxide molecule.

?

At first a handful then a number of students converted to Winboism in sympathy for Edgar Malroy's plight. Towards the end about a third of the student population had run on the spot, at least half-heartedly.

Edgar Malroy held services in the grounds of the college at the most ridiculous times. He told his congregation that only men with red hair and two older sisters had souls. He told them that the universe was shaped like a vagina. He told them yellow was a better colour than green. He told them God was a just being who didn't like beekeepers, or jelly.

He slept with nearly half the girls on campus.

Then a group of Winbo supporters insisted on starting their praying with their left feet, instead of their right.

Eventually the sect became fully independent, accusing Edgar of being a false prophet.

The 'Lefters', as they became know, were still going strong years later, mostly in Gloucester, although a few had settled in Hull by 2024.

Then everyone went home for the vacation and Edgar Malroy was informed that he had failed his first year. He had run on the spot every three minutes during his exams and was not encouraged to sit retakes in the summer.

'I learned one thing though at Tewkesbury,' Edgar Malroy used to say. 'People sure are nuts.'

Edgar Malroy then went and had a passage of Nietzsche's *Twilight of the Idols* tattooed on his left buttock.

?

Sophia Alderson, when fully recovered, left Lourdes and returned to London where she became a taxi driver. Whenever anyone got in her taxi she would ask them where they were going, heaven or hell. There were hundreds of bibles in the back seat of Sophia's taxi.

Sophia Alderson claimed, a week after starting work as a taxi driver, to have picked up the Virgin Mother in Sloane Square and taken her to the Ideal Home Exhibition at Earls Court. By that point 324 men had fallen in love with Sophia after they had climbed into her cab. They all became Christians.

Thirteen loved Sophia so much they became priests.

Four were so crazy about her they were monks within weeks.

Two months later, after Sophia had been given the sack from her cab company, at three in the morning on the 19th of August, in her tiny bedsit, the Virgin again appeared to Sophia. 'She was standing in front of me, a yard or two away, her hands together in prayer. She had a Walkman on but I couldn't hear any music.'

The Virgin told Sophia all the things that meant you went to hell. Sophia took notes.

?

I had not been back to the Metaphysical Betting Shop for nearly three months. I had though watched Edgar's commercials on the portable TV our floor manager kept in his office.

The commercials showed Edgar in front of the Metaphysical Betting Shop. The question mark on the spire now flashed in neon.

He wore a cheap suit. He kept on pointing at the camera. This is the sort of thing he said:

'Edgar Malroy here, inviting all of you with a religious or mystical inclination to pop into the Metaphysical Betting Shop and place a bet. You believe in something you can't prove, something beyond sensory experience? Then why not come in and make a bet here, at the Metaphysical Betting Shop? What have you got to lose? Come on, I dare you. Show me just how faithful you are. Put your money where your metaphysics are.'

Then a voice-over gave the location of the Metaphysical Betting Shop, while the camera zoomed unsteadily in on the flashing question mark.

A catchy tune would play then, and a warning would flash on the screen saying that you had to be over eighteen to bet.

'Put your money where your metaphysics are' was Edgar Malroy's little slogan. It was all over the place, at bus stops, on billboards, in the papers.

The Metaphysical Betting Shop was making a fine American profit.

22

Edgar Malroy gave each of his customers a badge which said:

I've put my
money where my
metaphysics are

You could also buy baseball caps and T-shirts with the slogan on.

Inside the Metaphysical Betting Shop hundreds of people were arguing about all sorts of things. Some had placards, some had books from which they were quoting vigorously, others meditated or prayed, most though were shouting and waving receipts of metaphysical bets they had made. Everyone was wearing their 'I've put my money where my metaphysics are' badges.

At the far end of the church, where the altar should have been, was a row of booths behind which sat pretty young girls.

The pretty young girls were wearing white swimsuits and on each of their heads, bouncing to and fro, was a furry pink question mark.

I moved into the throng of people. I was pushed this way and that as if I were some sort of inanimate object.

I tried to mention my bet on the existence of God but everyone ignored me, partly because I was a supermarket trolley but also because I was not wearing my 'I've put my money where my metaphysics are' badge.

I had left it in the supermarket.

If anyone asked one of the pretty girls with the pink furry question marks on their heads whether they believed in original sin, or whether they thought that the Holy Spirit proceeds from the

Father only, or that the Absolute has no qualities, or that Shree Shajanand Swami was a reincarnation of the God Vishnu, or that Shamans make people better by bringing their souls back to their bodies, or that circumcision was essential for entry into heaven, or that God inspired the prophets of the Old Testament, every one of the pretty girls would smile and then they would say this and only this:

'Who knows?'

It was in their contracts.

23

On the floor of the Metaphysical Betting Shop written in a circle were the following words of Friedrich Nietzsche:

> 'Metaphysics, the science . . . which deals with the fundamental errors of mankind – but as if they were the fundamental truths.'
>
> Human, All Too Human, p. 18

I pushed myself over to the betting booths, listening to the pretty girls typing away on their computers, taking money, handing out receipts and badges, smiling, shrugging and saying over and over again, 'Who knows?' 'Who knows?'

And then there was Edgar Malroy, sitting in a booth taking money from a man who believed that to be is to be perceived.

For some reason Edgar recognised me instantly.

'The theist supermarket trolley,' he said and smiled.

Then he said, 'Do you know what the Reverend Jim Jones said to the nine hundred people he ordered to kill themselves in Jonestown, Guyana, in 1978?'

I didn't.

Edgar Malroy said that Jim Jones had said this: 'Please for God's sake let's get on with it.'

He really did.

Then Edgar Malroy asked if I still believed in God.

I told him that I did.

Edgar laughed.

Then he suggested we both become members of the Universal Life Church. It was the only religion Edgar ever admired.

He called a pretty girl over and told her to take his place at the booth. She started to listen to a man who believed that the perfect circle existed outside of space and time.

When the man had finished gesturing with his finger he asked her what she thought. She smiled, sighed slightly and said very happily, 'Who knows?'

Edgar Malroy pushed me through the mass of people, smirking and nodding. He must have said 'Who knows?' thirty times before we were in his office.

The Universal Life Church, the only religion Edgar Malroy ever admired, was founded by Torby J. Hensley in 1976 in New York to provide a mail order ordination service, thus allowing the recipients of his mailed dog collars to classify their homes as churches and thereby save on tax payments.

It was the only religion Edgar Malroy ever admired.

I told Edgar when we were in his office that I didn't want to become a member of the Universal Life Church. I told him I knew absolutely, without a shadow of a doubt, that God existed.

Edgar laughed again, went over to his altar/desk and picked up a funny-looking device rather like a bar-code reader.

'What is it?' I asked.

'It's a Geiger counter. Notice how the needle doesn't move. How would you explain that?'

'There's no radiation in here?'

'There are no batteries in it. That, if you ask me, is Metaphysics, it's all – '

Edgar Malroy was about to explain what he meant, was about no doubt to mention the Guessing Hypothesis and the Linguistic Relativity Hypothesis, when there was a whining noise.

It sounded, in hindsight, like a 75mm recoilless cannon being fired from the block of flats across the road by Sophia Alderson.

One second before the shell smashed through the stained-glass window and exploded in Edgar Malroy's office, Edgar Malroy's watch started to beep.

This is what was on the liquid crystal display:

You are about to die.

24

In the ambulance, Edgar Malroy explained what he called his Guessing Hypothesis. I kept telling him to rest but he insisted.

Edgar Malroy had serious injuries to his left arm and leg.
 Edgar Malroy had also lost an eye.

In the end there were hundreds of attempts on his life. I was with him when many of the later attacks took place. I was not present of course at the very end.

Anyway, Sophia Alderson was the only would-be killer that Edgar Malroy confessed to loving. He even loved her after she made her second attempt on his life.

?

'There may be another plane of existence, an invisible higher order, a God, or whatever, but even if there is we can say nothing of it, can know nothing of it.'

'Rest, Edgar.'

'But you see that, don't you? . . . The metaphysical realm is totally inaccessible. It is beyond comprehension, so is it sensible to talk about it? Is it?'

'Rest.'

'Surely it is more sensible to shut up about it, quit wasting our time over it . . . The good news is we don't have to hurt our heads trying to believe the crap any more.'

At this point I lost my patience.

'But how do you know that the metaphysical realm cannot be known, Edgar? How can you be so sure we are so ignorant? By claiming that the metaphysical realm is unknowable aren't you claiming paradoxically to know something about the metaphysical realm?'

'So that in effect I am saying all metaphysical assertions are impossible, including this one?'

'Yes.'

'No. I don't claim to know that we can't know anything about the metaphysical realm.'

'What are you claiming then?'

'That we can't know that we know. When you make a metaphysical claim I don't say it's wrong, I don't say it is false. All I say is, Who knows? All I am saying is we don't know that it is right. I'm not saying that all metaphysical claims are false, only that they could be. What do you call it when you suggest something but you don't know you are right?'

I didn't know.

'A guess. That is what I maintain all metaphysics are: wild guesses. With wild guesses there is absolutely no logical reason to believe one is more likely to be right than any other and do you know how many wild metaphysical guesses mankind has made over the centuries, in the various cultures he has created?'

'No.'

'Neither do I, but I know this, it's an utterly ridiculous number.'

?

Edgar Malroy was then taken into St Antony's hospital where he was anaesthetised and asked to count backwards from one hundred.

He got to eighty-eight before passing out.

Just before he did pass out, I told Edgar I would pray to God for him. And I did. I was a nut.

25

While Edgar Malroy recovered in hospital, Sophia Alderson gave herself up to the police. A 56 Chevy had apparently screeched to a stop outside Sophia's bedsit and the Virgin Mother had stepped out and shouted, in the most angelic voice Sophia had ever heard, the following words:

'Give yourself up, kid!'

So she did. The police officers who arrested Sophia when she walked into Tottenham Court Road station fell helplessly in love with her and told their wives that night that Jesus had died for the sins of mankind. In the end Sophia was taken to a mental institution on the outskirts of London known as Rainthrope House. Edgar Malroy used to say that in another era she would have been made a high priestess. In 2023 she was merely made to play bridge with the other patients. She played beautifully.

?

Edgar Malroy would never be able to walk without the aid of a stick again. In addition, in his case, a blink would be a lot like a wink.

?

Just two months after he became Pontiff, Pope John John issued an encyclical claiming that not only was there a rational argument for the existence of a God but there were in fact fourteen quite distinct rational arguments, all of which were up to the job. He unfortunately did not specify in the encyclical what these arguments were. It was in this encyclical that he also forbade the use of flashes on cameras.

?

Edgar Malroy's watch had not gone off as a warning about the recoilless cannon fired by Sophia Alderson. Edgar Malroy's watch went off every fifteen minutes or so reminding Edgar that he was finite, that he would die, and that he ought consequently to live for the moment.

26

When Edgar came out of intensive care I told him I had prayed for him. He said, 'Thanks for nothing.'

I gave Edgar some grapes and he started going on about what he called the Linguistic Relativity Hypothesis.

'The metaphysician, the priest, the nutter, thinks words are things,' he said. 'They are not, they're just words. Words give us the sensation of having described something or having found something, in fact they are just arbitrary labels and nothing to do with reality. The metaphysician has created God with mere words. Is reality English? Of course it isn't!'

Edgar had a grape.

'There is no good reason to think language, any language, mirrors the real world. We are trapped in our languages. Completely and totally trapped. A language in relation to its speaker is outside the speaker's reference. We can't talk about language just as you can't use a tool to fix itself.'

Edgar had another grape.

'The way we see the world is arbitrary, not set in stone; it is dependent on a mere agreement to organise in one way rather than another. Our language spheres are not products of the real world. Language does not express nature's nature in its grammar. We have made our languages up. You see what that means?'

I didn't.

'It means we are talking shit!'

Edgar had another grape.

'Despite their spelling, the word and the world are not intimately acquainted. As a matter of fact they may well never have met! The metaphysician cuts everything up according to his language, things become either/or. The metaphysician plants letters on the moon, he colonises space with words. It is one small step for man, one giant, impossible, leap for language. Everything is neatly divided up into word categories like the Absolute and mere perception, Heaven and Hell.

'The metaphysician has infected reality with the dualism found within his language. He has attempted to grammatise the world. He imposes on the world linguistic distinctions. He cuts. Snip snip snip goes the metaphysician.'

Edgar blinked or winked, then had another grape.

'The metaphysician smashes words on the world. He claims the world echoes his words when all we can really hear is silence.'

Edgar put his good hand to his ear and froze for a moment, then shouted so loudly that he accidentally removed the drip from his arm and fell out of bed.

What Edgar Malroy had shouted as he fell out of his bed was this: 'Language has raped the world!'

When the nurses had Edgar back in bed, and had reinserted his drip, they tried to insist that I leave and let Edgar rest.

Edgar said he hadn't finished yet.

'The metaphysician masturbates with words but thinks he is having an intimate relationship with the real world. He is carried along by his grand, unfounded assumption that reality is written in his language.'

With that Edgar Malroy passed out. He remained deeply committed to both his Guessing and Linguistic Relativity Hypotheses for the whole of his short life. I was confident back then that both hypotheses were utterly false.

?

Just as I was about to leave Edgar unconscious in his hospital bed he woke up, grabbed hold of my push-bar with his good arm and asked me if it was possible to disagree with someone violently, absolutely, to consider them immoral and nuts and yet still love them.

I told him I thought it was a long shot.

27

In 2023 Pope John John took time off from his busy film schedule and visited over twenty countries. It was on this whistle-stop tour that the world was shown the new Popemobile, the Popemobile for the late 2020s, according to the Vatican press release. Built from an old Soviet intercontinental nuclear missile carrier, the Popemobile weighed 340 tons and had a top speed of thirty miles per hour.

In place of a XMA12 Deathdealer missile, on the back of the Popemobile sat a massive thirty-foot cross which could be raised into an upright position.

The giant cross was filled with nearly twenty thousand gallons of holy water which was sprayed all around the Popemobile to a distance of two hundred yards.

The cockpit itself was for some reason from a US TomCat fighter plane. There were two seats: a driver sat in the front, and the Pope, a little cramped, sat in what had originally been the navigator's position.

From this position the Pope could pray, wave at the adoring crowds, lower and raise the giant crucifix, and turn on and off the holy water sprinklers.

During the 2023 tour, the giant Popemobile was normally surrounded by three hundred priests, four hundred nuns, three hundred members of various religious orders, three hundred and fifty members of the Central Security Office, and two hundred poleaxe-armed Swiss Guards, all jogging along trying to keep up with the Pope.

Every one of the priests, the nuns, the members of the various religious orders, the security men and the Swiss Guards wore yellow mackintoshes on account of the holy water the Pope would spray in various directions when the urge took him.

?

A month after Sophia Alderson's first attack Edgar Malroy took his 100,000th bet. It was made by a Bob Fairclough for the sum of £12 and was that the origin of all motion in the universe, an origin that is itself unmoved, was God.

28

It was around this time that a new soft drink was put on the market. It was called Pope Pop and distributed by the Vatican. Pope Pop was essentially just a normal cola consisting of carbonated water, sugar, colouring, phosphoric acid, flavourings and caffeine, but five per cent of total volume, according to the table of contents, was holy water from Rome.

On every can of Pope Pop was the following piece of advice: Best served repentantly.

As part of the sales strategy Pope John John was seen drinking from a can of Pope Pop as he gave his Christmas address in St Peter's Square.

On the day that Pope Pop came on to the market an estimated thirty-four million devout Catholics bought at least one four-pack.

?

On 12th of May 2023 the Archbishop of Canterbury and Primate of All England made a high profile visit to the Metaphysical Betting Shop. Edgar Malroy greeted the archbishop at the steps and walked with him into the ancient building. There Edgar Malroy waited patiently while the archbishop wrote out a cheque for the sum of £2,500 and with it bet that all thirty-nine Articles of the Church of England were true. After that Edgar Malroy gave the Archbishop of Canterbury an 'I've put my money where my metaphysics are' badge, and a complimentary baseball cap with the same slogan on.

Outside, the archbishop was asked by reporters what he thought of the Metaphysical Betting Shop.

He said he was glad the former Church property hadn't been turned into an estate agency or a camping shop as so much former Church property had.

When a reporter asked Edgar Malroy for his reaction to the archbishop's visit he said, 'The archbishop is always welcome here. We want nuts of all shapes and sizes.'

As the archbishop's motorcade drove off, Edgar and four of his female staff waved from the steps of the Metaphysical Betting Shop.

The archbishop had promised to come again.

The whole thing was mentioned on the six o'clock news that night, and a picture of the archbishop being kissed by two pretty young ladies in white swimsuits with furry pink question marks bouncing to and fro on their heads appeared in *The Times* the next day.

After the archbishop left, the Metaphysical Betting Shop took another 2,305 bets before closing for the night.

29

One of the Sunday papers ran a feature on Edgar Malroy, his Metaphysical Betting Shop, the Riverside siege in which his family had been wiped out and the recent assassination attempt by Sophia Alderson.

When he was asked about Miss Alderson, all Edgar Malroy would say was this:

'She's a little mixed up but she means well really.'

Edgar Malroy was also asked what the strangest metaphysical bet he had ever taken had been.

Edgar said that he had once written out an £500,000 IOU for a supermarket trolley betting on the existence of God.

The Chief Rabbi Dr David Hollick made a visit to the Metaphysical Betting Shop and spent £500 on the bet that Life is a gift of God and is to be lived in utter obedience to God for its fullest consummation.

A week later there was another high profile visit to the Metaphysical Betting Shop; the head of the Methodists Dr Brian Jones and a number of his ministers spent the morning being shown around, talking to the pretty women that worked behind the booths, sipping cups of coffee and betting a total of £3,000 of Church funds on various nutty things.

There was another photo call outside the Metaphysical Betting Shop and Edgar was photographed shaking Dr Jones' hand and smiling, holding in his other hand the cheque made out to the Metaphysical Betting Shop for £3,000.

Edgar Malroy said of Dr Jones that he was one of the nicest nuts he had met.

?

Muslim clerics from all over the country began requesting audiences with Edgar Malroy and spent larger and larger sums of money on bets.

Leaders of the Hindu religion followed. To everyone Edgar Malroy was a polite and courteous host, smiling, shaking hands and making sure everyone was having a good time. He told everyone who placed a bet that he thought them to be quite nuts but told them this in such a nice way people let it pass.

?

So many religious leaders felt obliged to call into the Metaphysical Betting Shop that newspaper and TV crews set up semi-permanently outside on the grass amid the thirty-five species of counted wild flowers.

Edgar Malroy made sure that the media was well looked after, sending a number of his girls out to them with cups of coffee and slices of fruit cake.

Edgar Malroy himself became a little media sensation.

Two days before the Summer Solstice the head Druid made an appearance at the Metaphysical Betting Shop. Edgar took his money and told him what he thought of him. After that seven chieftains of the Sotho-Tswana people, who had flown in especially from Southern Africa to make their bet, spent £3,045 on the bet that Modimo is one, supreme, the owner and master of all, invisible and intangible.

The next day a delegation of Japanese Shinto priests flew in and bet £3,500 that the two mysterious powers of nature, Kami Izanagi and Kami Izanami, created the terrestrial world, and the Sun God Amaterasu.

A week later over two hundred Lamas from Tibet, who had

organised a coach trip all the way to the Metaphysical Betting Shop, spent a total of £19,000.

This coach trip was followed by a very high profile visit by the sixteenth Dalai Lama on the 8th of September 2023.

?

Edgar tried to visit Sophia in her mental institution but she refused to see him. Edgar took this badly and had to cancel a lucrative meeting with thirty-two American Baptist ministers.

?

The sixteenth Dalai Lama bet £6,000 that there is no self lying behind the constituent parts of a person.

When Edgar Malroy handed the Dalai Lama his badge, and its message was translated for him by one of his followers, the Dalai Lama found it so funny that he collapsed in a heap on the floor and an ambulance was called. The incident was in all the papers and really put Edgar's betting shop on the map.

The Dalai Lama had laughed so hard at George Milles Jr's funeral that his false teeth had fallen out.

The Dalai Lama got better.

?

Towards the end of his 2023 tour, Pope John John even made a visit to Edgar's Metaphysical Betting Shop.

This is what happened:

The Popemobile, barely able to squeeze down the street, came to an abrupt stop outside the Metaphysical Betting Shop, the cockpit canopy was opened and the Pope leapt onto the road, undoing as he did so the World War II leather flying helmet he was wearing.

It was at this moment that the three hundred priests, four hundred nuns, three hundred members of various religious orders, three hundred and fifty members of the Central Security Office and two hundred poleaxe-armed Swiss Guards, not to mention the hundreds of devout Catholics and the media, caught up with the Popemobile. Everyone was wearing yellow mackintoshes.

The Pope ran up the steps of the Metaphysical Betting Shop and was greeted at the entrance by Edgar Malroy who was leaning against the door frame. He was wearing a T-shirt that had written on it, 'There is no game in the world like pursuing men, to save them.'

They stepped inside and the Pope made his £25,000 bet in one minute flat and was running down the steps of the ancient church to the Popemobile, a path being made for him by the priests, nuns, security men and Swiss Guards through the press, the adoring Catholics and the curious public.

There was a backward wave to Edgar Malroy, then Pope John John fastened his flying helmet back on his sacred head and sped off.

He had a tight schedule.

And after him raced the multitude of people completely drenched with holy water.

It was at this point, with the grounds of the Metaphysical Betting Shop almost empty of the Pope's supporters, that Sophia Alderson, who had been allowed out of Rainthrope House to see the Pope, made her second attempt on Edgar Malroy's life.

30

The floor manager gave me compassionate leave to visit Edgar in hospital.

'Well, here we are again,' said Edgar Malroy, sitting up in bed in St Antony's with a stupid grin on his face.

We talked for a while about religion and Geiger counters with no batteries in. We agreed to differ.

Then Edgar talked about Sophia. Edgar asked me if I thought Sophia loved him.

'Who knows, Edgar?' I said. 'Who knows?'

?

Sophia Alderson had fired on fully automatic. In total she had fired eight rounds. Five rounds had missed Edgar altogether, two had gone through the side of his stomach, but the last round had gone clean through the centre of Edgar Malroy's right hand, which was resting on the stone pillar by the doorway.

Sophia Alderson had fired at Edgar with an old Chinese rifle, modelled on the Soviet AK47 and used for a time by the Tamil Tigers.

Sophia Alderson swore that the world was made in seven days and that during her second attempt on Edgar's life the Virgin Mother had been sending her detailed instructions by flag from a council flat some two miles away.

Was she?
Who knows?

31

Pope John John, moments before the second attempt on Edgar's life, had bet £25,000 that he was God's messenger etc etc.

?

A week after Edgar had taken Pope John John's bet the Second Great Schism began.

It happened like this:

Pope John John bungee-jumped as usual from the Sistine Chapel ceiling and returned to his study where he rejected the thirty-two-page draft text prepared for him by Cardinal Philips on the issue of birth control.

Instead he published a document called *Humanae Vitae II*. Written in his own hand, with an HB pencil, *Humanae Vitae II* would become one of the most controversial documents in the history of the Roman Catholic Church.

32

Edgar Malroy opened the second Metaphysical Betting Shop in Belfast, on the Falls Road, a short distance from the headquarters of the Presbyterian and Methodist Churches. As the doors were opened, hundreds of Protestants and Catholics were queuing up outside.

Edgar Malroy made more money in the first day of bet-taking in Northern Ireland than he normally made in a month in London.

?

Humanae Vitae II rewrote the Vatican's view on birth control. *Humanae Vitae II* stated that contraception was acceptable in God's eyes provided that the condom used was itself sanctified.

?

After opening the Northern Ireland Metaphysical Betting Shop, Edgar set up the Doubt Fund. At a press conference he explained that from now on he would be putting thirty per cent of the profits of his two Metaphysical Betting Shops into the fund and donating the money to worthy causes. He began by buying St Antony's maternity ward four brand new incubators.

He also started providing food on Sunday mornings outside his London betting shop for the homeless and down-and-outs on the sole condition that they didn't talk about God.

?

Sophia Alderson found references to Edgar in her Bible, particularly the Book of Revelations. Edgar Malroy was rather popular in the Book of Revelations. According to Sophia Alderson, she had found no less than thirteen references to him.

Edgar had been less than ten feet away from Sophia when she discovered that the Book of Revelations referred to him.

For Edgar had begun making secret visits to her mental institution to watch her behind a one-way mirror with a Dr Cunningham. Most of the time the two men stood behind the one-way mirror Sophia Alderson would be deep in prayer. Often Sophia Alderson prayed for eight hours non-stop. She prayed beautifully.

Whenever Sophia Alderson prayed, Edgar got a tiny erection. As did Dr Cunningham. They were both in love with the nut.

Every time Sophia Alderson prayed and he found himself with a tiny erection Dr Cunningham would tick his clipboard.

'Good. Good,' he would say sometimes.

Outside the mental institution a small picket of nuts had gathered with illegible handwritten placards.

The nuts with their illegible handwritten placards jeered and booed at Edgar Malroy's car, which had customised number plates, whenever it drove past. The nuts outside Rainthrope House believed that Sophia Alderson was God's messenger etc etc.

Edgar's number plate read:

WHOKNOWS

Edgar always grinned whenever he drove past the picket, for each and every one of the placard holders wore an 'I've put my money where my metaphysics are' badge.

33

It was about this time that I visited Edgar again and told him of my intention to climb Mount Everest.

He didn't flinch. Though when I told him I also intended to meditate on God's existence and find a proof for him while pushing my way up Everest, he burst out laughing. He laughed like this:

Ahh-ooo. Ahh-ooo.

A ray of sunshine came through the stained-glass window which had been repaired after Sophia Alderson's first attempt on Edgar Malroy's life.

The stained-glass window which had originally shown St George killing the dragon now had a giant blue question mark on a white background.

The stained-glass window was also now bulletproof.

I told Edgar if I had time to think about it properly I was sure a proof of God would come to my Infinity Chip.

Edgar laughed out loud again and banged his left fist on his desk a number of times.

'Nuts have been searching for a proof of God's existence for thousands of years. There isn't one. Reason isn't behind your belief in God, reason isn't really behind anyone's belief in God. It's faith, completely blind faith. What I do here, my occupation, the taking of metaphysical bets, is the practical demonstration of just how nutty you people are. Do you know what blind faith is? After what happened to my family I gave this question a lot of thought. When Winboism, the cult I made up for a joke in my college days, became a recognised religion with an estimated twenty thousand believers, I gave it some more thought. When I discovered it was possible to take large sums of money off the religiously inclined, I wondered some more. What, when you pull away all the bullshit, all the lies, is at the heart of the religious endeavour? What is it that makes the nut tick?'

Edgar, getting quite excited, began pushing me around the room.

'I'll tell you. Desire. Blind faith is just the desire for something to be the case. The only thing that guides us in metaphysics is our desire, and thus blind faith is nothing but concealed wish-fulfilment. You believe in your funny God for one reason: you want to believe. Having blind faith in God is no different to saying that you would like it very very much if there was a God. But, my little theist shopping conveyance, the fact that you would like it very very much if there was a God makes not a squidgen of a difference to whether there actually is a God, does it? Not a squidgen. It doesn't change things one little bit. So you want a God, to give life meaning, well so fucking what?

'And that's not all, I'm afraid. Not that that isn't bad enough of course, but your blind faith in your funny God will, if I am not very much mistaken, push you slowly down the kaleidoscope-coloured furry slide of madness.'

Edgar stood up. 'Confusing a wish with a belief, you see, blurs the distinction between desires and reasons and invariably leads to insanity. I should know. I've seen some really bad cases. The light in their eyes has gone out. It's all very sad. Tragic really. Really religious people look as if they have been masturbating like billy-o. They even walk funny, the really bad nuts, they – '

At this point I told Edgar Malroy to shut up. I told him he was wrong about my belief in God. I told him I would find a proof of God on Mount Everest, a cast-iron, impregnable reason for my belief in God, and Edgar would have to admit he had made the biggest mistake of his life.

It was then that Edgar told me about Maurice Wilson and arranged for me to fly to the Himalayas.

I left the next day.

ShopALot reported me stolen.

?

Maurice Wilson was born in Bradford, Yorkshire, in 1898. During World War I he was shot twice by a German machine gun in the third battle of Ypres.

One bullet hit his left arm, the other bullet punctured his lung. The wound made a sssssssssss noise as his right lung collapsed.

He got better.

?

The inventor of the machine gun, Dr R. Gatling, also invented a machine for sowing rice, and it was from this rice-sowing machine that he got the idea for the machine gun.

?

Maurice Wilson believed that if you fast for thirty-five days, subsisting on sips of water, and pray to God, then you could do anything. He attempted to climb Mount Everest to publicise this belief.

His plan was to crash-land a plane on the side of Everest and walk the rest of the way to the summit.

He took off from the London Aero Club, flew rather badly across Europe and the Middle East, and finally arrived in India where the local authorities promptly impounded his plane, regarding him as a maniac.

Then the monsoon came. Wilson fasted for thirty-five days, subsisting on sips of water, and prayed to God. At the end of the thirty-five days of fasting Wilson felt incredibly weak, got a cold and decided to go home.

?

The metaphysical betting business went from strength to strength.

If a nut could think it up, and if it couldn't be proven one way or the other, Edgar Malroy would take the bet.

The poor girls who worked at the booths occasionally experienced what Edgar termed Metaphysical Burn-Out or MBO, with symptoms rather like a migraine, but far worse. When a burn-out took place the booth would be closed and the girl would be carried on a special stretcher to a staff room where she would be coached back to normality by Edgar Malroy, who had developed a special technique for dealing with MBO cases. He called the technique the Errrr. Often the Errrr was so successful that the MBO victim would be back at her booth in a few hours. Those cases that proved to be more serious were looked after in a special care centre Edgar had set up near Brighton.

There was an average of one serious MBO a week. This sort of figure was hardly surprising given the metaphysical nonsense the staff of the two betting shops were exposed to.

Looking back, it was pathetic. Even at this point there were a few cases of the metaphysicians themselves suffering from MBO and this led Edgar Malroy to form Metaphysical Betting Anonymous, an informal group that in the early days numbered less than a dozen, met with Edgar at 4.30 on Tuesdays and discussed their obsession with meaningless assertions.

34

Maurice Wilson changed his mind about going home. Instead of crash-landing on the mountain he decided to climb all the way up Mount Everest on foot.

He travelled illegally over the Tibetan uplands and on the 30th of May 1933 began his ascent.

Maurice Wilson, a very serious religious nut, who thought that if you fast for thirty-five days, subsisting on sips of water, and pray to God, you could do anything, froze to death 250 feet up Mount Everest.

Aloha.

Edgar assured me that this story was perfectly true.

?

Cardinal Philips always liked to spend at least fifteen minutes each afternoon at the piano, which he had unfortunately never learned to play.

Cardinal Philips continued with this habit when he became the most powerful cardinal in Rome as the head of the Congregation of the Doctrine of the Faith, that is to say the Inquisition.

Cardinal Philips had been sat some seven minutes in front of his piano when one of his officials entered his office and promptly stubbed his toe on a radiator that reached out into the doorway.

The day he moved into the office, Cardinal Philips had workmen move the radiator into the doorway so that he could see if any of his underlings would take the Lord's name in vain when they collided with the metal.

The repositioning of the radiator meant of course that the cardinal could not close his door, but this had not troubled him, giving him the opportunity to observe the behaviour of his underlings at their desks.

On this particular day the official walked into the radiator and mumbled under his breath the word 'Mamma' and although this made Cardinal Philips' eyebrow rise somewhat he decided to drop the matter, as the priest had not said Holy Mamma or Blessed Mamma; if he had done so it would have been quite a different matter.

Cardinal Philips did not turn around, he sat perfectly still in front of his piano. The official hovered in the centre of the room for a moment then boldly walked up to the cardinal and leaning over his shoulder gently rested the piece of paper he held in his hand in front of the upside-down sheets of Mozart on the piano. Cardinal Philips snatched the piece of paper up and without looking at it waved it at the official who immediately retreated to the centre of the room.

'Brother Howe, what is this, a confession? I am busy, as you can see. I am spending fifteen minutes of this afternoon, as I do every afternoon, in front of my piano, and I do not wish to be disturbed.'

Cardinal Philips glanced at the piece of paper, a photocopy of a page of almost illegible handwriting, and read part of it absentmindedly.

Then he stood up, clutched the document with both hands and read it carefully again. Then he shouted.

He shouted the following words:

'Holy Mamma!'

Then the cardinal put the piece of paper under his elbow, pulled up his cassock and rushed for the door where he hit his leg on the obtrusive radiator, fell backwards and hit his head on the piano. It released a few discordant notes before the cardinal dropped to the floor unconscious and bleeding profusely.

?

At the same time that Cardinal Philips received his blow to the head, Edgar Malroy flew to Jerusalem and presented plans for a £5 million Metaphysical Betting Shop in the heart of the Old City opposite the famous Wailing Wall.

Edgar Malroy made his plans public and told the Jerusalem press that 'From the very beginning I have wanted to come to Jerusalem. I know a number of nuts who regularly travel from the Middle East to the Metaphysical Betting Shop in London, and that many more nuts would do so if they could afford to. This is silly. If there is a nut anywhere in the world, I want to take his money from him with the minimum of inconvenience to him. Which is why I want to open a betting shop in this beautiful and very nutty city of yours.'

Edgar Malroy said that the proposed betting shop would employ some four hundred people recruited locally. It would also have facilities for disabled customers. Edgar Malroy said that in addition to the betting shop he would build a health care centre and a milk processing plant able to produce over two tons of dried milk a day, all of which he would give away to sick and poor children in and around Jerusalem. He would also hand out food at the proposed Metaphysical Betting Shop to the down-and-outs at weekends, provided no one talked about God.

Tony Bouttell, spokesman for Jerusalem City Council, told reporters that officials had only just received the plans and hoped to discuss them further at a meeting on the 16th of June.

Pleased with the early response, Edgar flew from Jerusalem to California and presented a similar proposal for a betting shop on thirty-five thousand square feet of land near Long Beach.

It was while Edgar Malroy was in the States that he was informed that his company had just taken its one millionth bet.

?

The millionth metaphysical bet to have been placed in one of the two newly opened betting shops was made by Yvonne Creed who bet £32.50 that hell is very hot.

Yvonne Creed became a minor celebrity and was interviewed in all the papers.

Edgar Malroy sent Yvonne Creed on an all expenses paid trip around the world on a cruise liner.

?

On the 2nd of June Edgar Malroy went public. His metaphysical betting business became known as Scepticism Inc. Ordinary shares were offered to anyone, except priests, at £8.50 each, and by the end of the first day of trading the price had shot up to £30. A block of one hundred shares purchased for £8,500 was worth more than £1,500,000 two years later.

Scepticism Inc. became one of the sixty companies that made up the FTSE.

?

On the same day the Virgin Mother appeared to Sophia Alderson. Again. She appeared in Sophia Alderson's room wearing a bee-keeper's outfit. She leaned over and whispered into Sophia's left ear, in a strangely South African accent, the date for the end of the world.

Imagine that.

35

Just two hours after *Humanae Vitae II* was published a number of cardinals denied that it had been written by the Pope.

A statement was issued by the Pope's secretary confirming that Pope John John had indeed been the author of *Humanae Vitae II*.

Some cardinals denied that the Pope's secretary had issued the statement confirming that Pope John John had written *Humanae Vitae II*.

A somewhat agitated representative of the Congregation of the Doctrine of the Faith suggested to journalists that there had been some minor errors made by clerks responsible for copying the document and that it would have to be withdrawn so that corrections could be made.

But half an hour later Pope John John told reporters personally that there had been no clerks involved, he had written the whole thing himself with an HB pencil. To reinforce this fact he drew the pencil from the breast pocket of his cassock and showed it to the cameras.

Cardinal Philips remained unconscious.

Word of *Humanae Vitae II* spread across the world and images of the HB pencil and Pope John John's finger pointing at it appeared on the front pages of newspapers and on TV.

Edgar Malroy saw the pencil on the evening news.

?

Sophia Alderson, soon after receiving her latest visitation from the Holy Mother of God, placed the red mark she had been saving for the end of the world on her wall chart.

At the first opportunity Sophia Alderson told Dr Cunningham that the end of the world was coming.

Dr Cunningham didn't hear what Sophia was saying. He was staring into her ridiculously beautiful eyes thinking about his clipboard which he had left in his office by mistake.

Sophia Alderson was the last patient Dr Cunningham would ever have.

She was also of course the most beautiful.

Pretty soon the group of protesters outside Rainthrope House, with their illegible placards and 'I've put my money where my metaphysics are' badges, heard the news that Sophia Alderson had been told the date for the end of the world.

They nodded and said told you so. They believed, you see, that Sophia Alderson was God's messenger etc etc.

Was she?

Who knows?

?

While all this was going on I was trying to scale the Khumbu icefall at the base of the western face of Everest, no easy task for a supermarket trolley.

As my ridiculously little wheels slipped and I skidded all over the place I thought about the ontological proof of God.

Existence according to the proof was part of the ingredients that went into making the Supreme Being.

Surely though, existence wasn't a property but a state; not something in a thing, but a state a thing is in.

The concept of God was no different if there was such an entity in existence or if there wasn't.

?

The number of metaphysical bets made grew and grew. A small army of entrepreneurs set up stalls outside the Metaphysical Betting Shops selling all manner of refreshments (including tangerines) to the constantly growing queues of nuts.

Everyone seemed to want to make at least one bet. It became something of a craze. The number of lottery tickets sold started to go down. Everyone bragged about their metaphysical assertions and anyone who didn't sport an 'I've put my money were my metaphysics are' badge was considered a social outcast. People began to show off their metaphysical bets in specially manufactured albums, available from the Metaphysical Betting Shops for a quite ridiculous price; on the cover of the albums was a giant question mark. Anyone who made over one hundred bets, each worth in excess of £100, was awarded a golden 'I've put my money where my metaphysics are' badge. Every bishop in the Church of England soon possessed such a badge, as did the leaders of over thirty major religions.

Parents began making bets for their children. Wills stated posthumous bets, invariably about the final destinations of the deceased. *The Times* printed bets in their personal column in between births and deaths. Priests bet on their sermons.

Billboards everywhere asked, 'Have you put your money where your metaphysics are today?' and Edgar's TV ads appeared at least six times a night.

As everyone had expected, for there would have been riots otherwise, Edgar was given permission to start building his new offices in Jerusalem and California. Work started almost immediately. Edgar planned to expand as rapidly as he could. He told his staff and shareholders that he wanted to have a Metaphysical Betting Shop within walking distance of every nut in the world. He said that he didn't want any nut to believe something metaphysical without being able to put money on it. 'I want them to think Edgar Malroy whenever they think something nutty, something metaphysical, and reach for their wallets.' That was, he said, his goal. He told this to reporters. He also told reporters of his plans to build a 400-metre-high tower in the centre of London. The tower, to be called Sceptic Tower, would be by far the tallest building in the capital and was to be the central headquarters of Edgar's growing worldwide metaphysical betting empire.

Plans for the tower were quickly drawn up and work on the foundations began almost immediately in the heart of London, next to the Bank of England.

Edgar wanted Sceptic Tower shaped like a question mark.

?

Around the same time as plans for the Sceptic Tower were released, representatives of Scepticism Inc. began buying up surplus stocks of powdered milk, wheat and butter from the United States and Europe. Edgar Malroy then spent in excess of ten million pounds buying up old cargo ships which were used to transport the surplus food to starving children in Africa and India.

Each of Edgar Malroy's ships was painted white and had giant question marks on its bow and stern.

36

There were no shops on the Khumbu icefall. There was no trace of human civilisation at all. There was nothing but snow, ice and a supermarket trolley in search of its maker.

?

When Cardinal Philips finally regained consciousness he found that he had lost his sense of smell. This fact did not bother him much; in fact he gave it only half a thought when his doctor told him.

The doctor said, 'I'm afraid your eminence has lost his sense of smell.'

The cardinal sniffed twice, to check, looked off into the distance, then spoke:

'The Lord,' said Cardinal Philips, 'works in mysterious ways, does he not, doctor?'

'Sure,' said the doctor.

Cardinal Philips ordered his cassock to be brought to him and, ignoring the doctor's protest, got a cab back to the Vatican where he demanded an audience with the Pope.

Cardinal Philips demanded that the Pope retract his stance on birth control.

The Pope said that it was God's will that *Humane Vitae II* be observed. The Pope's secretary then reminded his holiness that he was due in ten minutes at the preview of his latest film, *Noah*.

Cardinal Philips left the Pope's study rubbing his head and rushed to his office where eighteen cardinals were screaming and shouting about the Holy Spirit and the need to call a General Council.

At 4.30 Cardinal Philips ordered the other cardinals out into the hallway. Then Cardinal Philips sat in front of his piano for fifteen minutes. During this time the other cardinals stood just outside his room and twiddled their thumbs.

When the fifteen minutes were up, Cardinal Philips rose from his piano, called the other cardinals back into his office and the screaming and shouting started again.

?

Sophia, two weeks after Mary had told her the date for the end of the world, had persuaded Dr Cunningham to rig up for her a loudspeaker system outside her second-storey window so that she could speak to the growing number of her followers at the gates.

Edgar Malroy was present when Sophia Alderson first used the loudspeaker system. He and Dr Cunningham stood behind the one-way mirror and watched as Sophia spoke to her followers. She spoke beautifully of course.

'The end of the world is near. The most blessed Mother of God has told me the date. Unless you obey God's will all will be destroyed. Beg for God's mercy. Stop swearing. Give up toast. Keep Sunday special. All the world's governments must obey God's ultimatum at top speed.'

'She asked for the loudspeaker system,' explained Dr Cunningham, ticking his clipboard ferociously. He then broke into tears. 'I'd . . . I'd give her anything she wanted.'

'I know what you mean,' said Edgar, looking at Sophia's perfect little ankles as she leaned out of her window shouting into her microphone with her pretty voice.

'Stop it, or else God will destroy the world. Stop swearing, stop picking your noses, stop wearing odd socks, stop looking at naked animals, we must make woollen trousers and jackets for all of God's animals, we should have done that a long time ago, stop telling jokes, especially knock-knock jokes, stop using microwaves on Sunday, it's obscene! Stop eating with your fingers, I mean it, stop belching, stop farting, stop lying and jumping the lights, bring back capital punishment and public flogging, stop having sex or thinking about sex, stop being slovenly. Stop drinking all alcoholic beverages, in fact stop drinking anything except carrot juice.

'The date is set. The end of the world is coming. Repent!'

Dr Cunningham sank to the floor of the observation room, his clipboard in his lap. He couldn't take any more. 'Her mind's all twisted and what have you, but when you get to know her as well as I do, its impossible not to love her. She's so beautiful. I mean, I see why those people out there think she is God's messenger etc etc, don't you?'

'Yes,' said Edgar, grabbing the doctor's clipboard and ticking it himself. 'She is beautiful. She is as beautiful as the stagnant pool out of which life arose.'

Sophia paused, her heavenly chest heaved, she drew strands of her golden hair out of her face with her perfect little hand.

When she spoke again into the microphone it was with a calmer voice. It was the purest, kindest voice anyone has ever heard.

'Who is the oldest amongst you?' she asked.

There was mumbling in the crowd; people shouted their ages. Eventually, a tiny little woman in a wheelchair was pushed to the gates. She looked back at the other followers, proud it seemed at being singled out.

'How old are you?' Sophia asked over the loudspeaker system.

'Ninety-two,' said the old lady.

'What?' said Sophia.

'Ninety-two,' said the old lady a little louder than before.

'What?'

'Ninety-two!' shouted a young man from the crowd.

'Ninety-two?' said Sophia, checking she had heard right.

'Yes,' the crowd shouted. 'Right.' There was a pause as Sophia began to pray. Then after a little while she spoke again.

'God has just told me that you will not have to wait long before you are by his side.'

The little old lady gasped and turned her head back to the crowd whom she stared at reproachfully as if it was all their fault.

There were gasps from the audience and shouts of hallelujah.

The old lady was wheeled back to the crowd and congratulated.

Sophia Alderson turned off the microphone then knelt down and began to pray directly in front of the one-way mirror. This proved too much for Dr Cunningham and Edgar had to help him back to his office.

On Dr Cunningham's desk was a dead cactus plant and Sophia Alderson's file which had been open on the doctor's desk for the last six months.

37

Sophia Alderson had begun writing down the content of her daily inspirations and visitations on a computer bought for her by Dr Cunningham.

The doctor had a photocopying machine installed in Sophia's room as well. It was one of those huge machines able to print over a hundred pages a go.

Edgar had remarked, when he saw the photocopier in action for the first time from behind the one-way mirror, 'She could take over a small country with one of those.'

Dr Cunningham exploded. 'I don't care!' he shouted.

Fortunately the observation room was soundproofed.

Sophia had to fold every single photocopied page she wanted to send to her followers into a paper airplane.

Folding every page into a paper airplane was such a laborious process that pretty soon she was making paper airplanes while she prayed.

On good days she was able to make fifty-five an hour.

Dr Cunningham had timed her.

Sophia Alderson would launch the paper planes one after the other out of the window as they were made, without looking, still deep in prayer. Only about half made it as far as the gates and the waiting group of followers.

Those paper planes that did get as far as the gates were fought over violently. Then they would be unfolded and read. As they read the paper planes Sophia's followers would nod and say told you so.

?

I turned to the teleological proof of God. It went like this: the idea of God was such a sublime and majestic concept that it simply couldn't have come from anything less sublime and majestic than God himself.

The proof seemed to rest precariously on a profound under-estimation of the power of imagination. Surely it was at least possible that mortals could come to the notion of God by seeing themselves as finite and then imagining what it would be like not to be limited in any sort of way.

Once such a possibility was accepted the 'proof' collapsed.

?

The Jerusalem Metaphysical Betting Shop was finished in just six weeks. It was the largest Metaphysical Betting Shop ever, with over one hundred and thirty booths and a coffee shop. The health care centre and milk processing plant were also opened. Over four thousand local women had applied to work at the betting shop, each filling out a questionnaire.

Edgar Malroy chose the prettiest women who, when asked what they thought life was all about on their questionnaires, had written two silly little words, namely Who Knows? or words to that effect. Anyone who wrote swear words on this part of the questionnaire were made managers.

At the opening ceremony of the third Metaphysical Betting Shop were the leaders of the city's Jewish, Muslim, Orthodox and Catholic communities, the mayor of Jerusalem and Israel's Minister for Religious Affairs. There were also representatives of the other religious faiths present in Jerusalem, which included the Anglican Church, the Lutheran Church, the Presbyterian Church, a number of Baptist Churches, the Christian Science Church, the Mormon Church, and the Seventh Day Adventist Church.

Literally hundreds of thousands of people crowded the plaza in front of the Wailing Wall and the Metaphysical Betting Shop as the opening ceremony was completed. Edgar Malroy put on free food and refreshments; ten thousand kosher hamburgers and kebabs were handed out and over fifty tons of oranges were freshly squeezed for the occasion.

The mayor of Jerusalem said:

'This is just the sort of thing we like to see.'

The first bets the Jerusalem office took were made by the leaders of the various religious communities, and were worth altogether £3.5 million.

When these bets were made a thousand silver balloons with

question marks printed on them were released from the roof of the betting shop and the booths were opened to the public.

All day business at the third Metaphysical Betting Shop was brisk as an estimated 200,000 Jews, Christians of various denominations, and Muslims queued up along the Wall to place their bets. Many had spent the night by the Wailing Wall to ensure they would be among the first to place a bet.

The police reported a total of six minor theological scuffles, and there were two cases of MBO.

By nine o'clock all the young girls working at the Metaphysical Betting Shop were half asleep. Attempts to close the betting shop for the night met with resistance, however, as thousands of nuts insisted on being allowed to continue placing bets.

By eleven o'clock the police were forced to disperse the crowd with tear gas and water cannon and the Metaphysical Betting Shop staff were finally able to close it for the night.

Everyone except Edgar went home.

The steps of the Metaphysical Betting Shop were strewn with the receipts of thousands and thousands of bets nuts had dropped when the area had been cleared by water cannon. They were like damp leaves. Edgar left his third betting shop, got down on his hands and knees and threw the receipts into the air.

He had made more then fifteen million pounds in a little under twelve hours.

In the morning even more nuts than the day before gathered to place bets at the third Metaphysical Betting Shop. They had come from far and wide. That night nuts yet again had to be cleared from the steps of the betting shop, money in hand, with water cannon so that staff could sleep. This went on for three days and nights until Edgar got permission from the City Council to open all night and began employing night staff.

38

On the 5th of September 2023 violent tidal waves ravaged the island of Madagascar. 3,450 people were killed, thousands more were made homeless. The first relief aid that reached the island was flown in on white airplanes with giant question marks on their fuselages.

When Edgar was questioned about the relief operation in Madagascar and the extent of the devastation all he would say was this: 'God works in fucking mysterious ways.'

?

Cardinal Philips presented the Pope with a letter regretting his new stance on artificial birth control. The letter was signed by 18 cardinals, 76 bishops, 34 professors, 1,305 priests, 102 theology teachers and a number of important lay Catholics.

The Pope read the letter, folded it neatly into a paper plane and threw it out of the window.

The next day Cardinal Philips and approximately half of the cardinals were absent from the Pope's morning bungee jump from the Sistine Chapel ceiling.
    There were correspondingly fewer claps and less 'Ooooos' as God's messenger etc etc bounced up and down. It brought him closer to God, he claimed.

?

The press began to fall in love with Sophia. However, Dr Cunningham refused to allow any reporter near her. In fact

Dr Cunningham only allowed himself, a few trusted nurses and the Virgin Mother near his beloved patient.

There was of course also Edgar Malroy. To Dr Cunningham's own surprise he found Edgar a sort of companion rather than a threat. From the first day they had met, when Edgar had limped into his office with the aid of a stick, wearing an eye patch, one arm in a sling and holding a ridiculously large bunch of flowers in his good hand, Dr Cunningham had known that Edgar Malroy, like himself, was hopelessly in love with his patient.

It had taken a few months for it to dawn on Dr Cunningham, but he now realised, much to his dismay, that he was actually jealous of all the attention Sophia Alderson had shown Edgar Malroy.

?

When the fourth Metaphysical Betting Shop was opened in California so many people came to place bets that traffic jams stretched for thirty-two miles in every direction; there were three cases of MBO and at least fourteen people died from carbon-monoxide poisoning.

?

It took me another two months to reach the top of the icefall. How I managed it no one, including myself, ever really found out. I was twenty thousand feet above sea level; the weather was perfect. I pushed myself upwards, I was a driven supermarket trolley.

?

The crisis in the Catholic Church caused by the publication of *Humanae Vitae II* worsened. An anonymous editorial in *The Universe* claimed that '*Rebellion is only a matter of time. The Pope cannot pretend to be surprised by it.*'

The Pope kept showing the world's press his HB pencil and saying that he didn't know what all the fuss was about.

He also began spending a great deal of time in the Vatican gardens where he claimed to have seen repeatedly the sun rotating wildly in the sky in much the same way that Pope Pius XII had witnessed back in 1950.

Events moved quickly. As dissent grew, a delegation of cardinals led by Cardinal Philips demanded another audience with the Pope.

This was eventually granted.

Cardinal Philips solemnly informed the blinking Pope that in his and his fellow cardinals' view the path the Pope had embarked upon seemed flatly to contradict the teaching and doctrine of previous Popes and that perhaps more to the point what he proposed was an act of extreme commercialism in terribly bad taste.

The Pope rubbed his eyes and informed the cardinals present that he had on the issue of contraception simply taken the 'long view', as had, he argued, Paul VI.

The Pope then gave a lecture about dwindling Church funds, the need to remain relevant in the modern world, and then, getting off the point, gave a most animated account of the latest solar miracle he had witnessed. When he had finished he slumped back into his chair and blinked slowly four times and then told Cardinal Philips that *Humanae Vitae II* would stand and that he could love it or leave it.

The Pope then took out of his breast pocket a prototype of the Vatican-sanctioned condom and showed it to the rebel cardinals.

On one side there was a picture of the Virgin Mother, which the Pope told them would glow in the dark, while on the other was a ribbed crucifix.

When Cardinal Philips and his supporters not only refused to turn off the lights so they could all see the Virgin Mother glow in the dark, but protested still further, Pope John John said he had had enough and had the rebel cardinals locked up in a fifteenth-century room.

However, the Cardinals climbed out of a sixteenth-century window.

39

Scepticism Inc. continued to expand rapidly. A Metaphysical Betting Shop was even opened in St Peter's Square in the Vatican. An estimated 500,000 Catholics queued in the square to place their bets the day it opened. On the morning of its opening Pope John John bet £25,000 on live TV that he was still God's messenger etc etc.

Another Metaphysical Betting Shop was opened in Mecca, inside the sacred mosque, about twenty metres from the Kabah itself. Over ten million pounds was spent on bets the first day the Mecca betting shop opened. Muslims made a series of bets as they circled the Kabah anti-clockwise seven times.

Another betting shop was opened in the Golden Temple in Amritsar, and made pre-tax profits of £1.2 million on its first day of business.

On the 6th of September Edgar Malroy took his one billionth bet. It was made by Robyn Moller and was for £125. The billionth bet was that a combination of seated meditation, counselling with Zen Masters and the use of paradoxical sayings leads to a realisation of supreme truth. Robyn Moller was given two luxury holiday homes and a life supply of toilet paper by Scepticism Inc.

During this time over five hundred prefabricated schools with their teachers strapped into their desks were dropped from white Scepticism Inc. helicopters in remote regions of the world.

200,000 new houses with running water were built for the poor in India, South America and Africa with money provided by Edgar Malroy's company.

Whole continents were inoculated against hundreds of diseases by doctors working for Scepticism Inc.

Thirty per cent of the World Heath Organisation and the UN Commission for Refugees funds came from Scepticism Inc.

Some thirty-two per cent of all money donated to registered charities came from Edgar's Doubt fund.

Over ten thousand cataract operations were performed for free by Scepticism Inc. medical teams each week.

Hospitals all over the globe received cash hand-outs, free incubators, EG scanners, and life-support machines, and employees of Scepticism Inc. continued to ship surplus stocks of basic food to those people who needed it most.

Edgar was made a national hero in over 120 countries. He was awarded more medals than anyone could count. 12,005.

He was even knighted by the King of England for his services to mankind.

40

Some fifteen thousand builders worked day and night on Sceptic Tower. They were paid triple their normal wages. Edgar Malroy wanted to move in by the end of the year.

?

I zig-zagged around crevasses, inched over rock faces and pushed myself through snow drifts. I also considered the causal proof of God. All things that happen have a cause; it followed, so the proof went, that there must have been a first cause and that first cause could only have been God.

Why, though, if everything else must have a cause, did God not have a cause? Wasn't it terribly convenient and arbitrary to stop the regress of causes at God?

There seemed to me, on the side of Everest, as good a reason to stop the causal regress at the world, one step before God, and say simply that the world did not require a cause. There was no logical reason to think that the universe cannot have been uncaused.

Who knows?

?

Dr Cunningham groomed himself carefully before every one of his sessions with Sophia Alderson. He spent a small fortune on different bow ties and glasses in the hope that one particular combination would prove irresistible to his patient.

He would do anything Sophia Alderson wanted him to. He was utterly powerless. Like countless others he had fallen for the beautiful nut.

During one of their regular sessions, Sophia told the doctor that producers were asking her to appear on various television chat shows.

'I know Cardinal Morris has told me I shouldn't open myself to the charge of publicity seeking, but The World has to know the Truth, does it not, Doctor?'

Dr Cunningham agreed as he always did. He would see what he could do. He ticked his clipboard.

Sophia Alderson prayed and it started to rain.

The rain washed all the ink off Sophia Alderson's followers' placards, but this hardly mattered for what they had written on them was illegible anyway.

?

On the 17th of September 2023 Popedoms were put on the market for the first time. They were on sale at all major supermarkets, including ShopALot. It was also possible to buy them from Catholic priests after confession.

Popedoms cost roughly five times the price of other condoms, but then the others did not have the Sin-Free Warranty that Popedoms came with.

Cardinal Philips said it was a sad day for the Church that things had come to this.

Even so over 300 million Popedoms had been bought by the time churches and supermarkets closed for the night on the 17th of September.

Sales would increase a hundredfold by the end of the week.

Within six months Rome would became the largest single producer of condoms in the world and the manufacture of sacred prophylactics would became Italy's single largest industry.

41

More and more Metaphysical Betting Shops were opened around the world.

When a Metaphysical Betting Shop was opened in downtown Beirut the Sunni and Shia Muslim communities competed desperately to spend the most money on their marginally different metaphysical beliefs.

The same thing happened with the Muslim and Christian communities in Sarajevo when Edgar Malroy opened one of his shops there.

?

By the time I turned to the cosmological proof I was twenty-two thousand feet above sea level and directly under the Lhotse face.

The cosmological proof of God went so – the world, the cosmos, required a sufficient reason for it to have come into being, a reason outside of the world. This would have to be a necessary being which contained its own sufficient reason, namely God.

Like the causal proof, the cosmological proof rested on an unwarranted assumption; must the universe have had a sufficient reason for existing?

Who knows?

If God could be self-sufficient why couldn't the universe?

One saw examples of sufficient reason and causation in the world, but applying these principles to the world as a whole was to go beyond the point of evidence. Just because something applies to the constituent parts, there was no guarantee that it would apply to the whole.

The cosmological proof, like the causal proof, failed utterly to get off the ground, in fact both proofs were profoundly question-begging and no more than expressions of nuts' desires for purposefulness to exist at an absolute level.

Just below the Lhotse face it would be fair to say that I had something of a spiritual crisis.

?

The Archbishop of Canterbury had by this stage made well over one hundred and twenty visits to the very first Metaphysical Betting Shop. He came at least once a week. He loved it. Some of his most senior advisers suggested caution but the archbishop would hear none of it and went on spending vast sums of Church money on metaphysical bets with great earnestness and seriousness. 'I believe therefore I bet,' he told reporters and boy, did he bet. On average the archbishop spent £100,000 every week. He really did.

He was not alone. Priests at every level of the Church of England queued up and bet like men possessed.

It is fair to say that they got a little carried away.

?

Edgar received approximately two hundred letters of thanks a day, from people whose lives had been improved in one way or another by the company's efforts. Edgar Malroy saw that each and every one who wrote to Scepticism Inc. with thanks was sent a standard reply letter.

The standard reply letter went like this:

We at Scepticism Inc. are glad to have helped in the small ways that we do. Our goal is the least pain and the longest life for as many as possible. We try. We believe solemnly in very little. We say: 'Believe less, more.' We don't believe very much. All we really believe in fact is this: People matter more than the Truth. We sing it to the heavens. We shout it from the rooftops.

Never forget, though, that all that we have managed to do so far simply wouldn't have been possible without all the nuts in the world who believe all kinds of nonsense they cannot know and insist on giving us the ridiculous sums of money they do for pieces of paper and silly little badges.

Thank God for the nuts!

Yours,

Edgar Malroy
An undevout astronomer.

42

The Pope, in an attempt to silence the growing chorus of disapproval over Popedoms, went on Italian state television and declared that any Catholic who found themselves in disagreement with his ruling on birth control should pray to God for enlightenment and not express their opinions until such enlightenment had taken place.

'Do not forget, my children, that I, his holiness the Pope, am far wiser and closer to God than you. Remember that the Church is smarter than you are. Do not follow your own opinions, follow mine. Mine are right. That is really the long and the short of it.' The Pope then crossed himself and walked off camera.

It was a brave performance. The Pope had looked like authority itself with his white cassock and his 'I've put my money where my metaphysics are' badge.

It was, though, not enough to stop the growing opposition to *Humanae Vitae II* within the Church.

On the 25th of September, the day after the Exaltation of the Holy Cross, Cardinal Philips, with the backing of a slim majority of cardinals, declared Pope John John insane and denounced his Papacy. Promptly after this announcement was made the rebel cardinals elected Cardinal Philips as the new Pope.

One of Philips' first acts as Pope was to forbid the use of Popedoms, the result of which was that half of Christendom didn't know if they were coming or going.

43

Pope John John reacted to the election of Cardinal Philips as Pope by excommunicating him and his rebel cardinals and releasing new family-sized packets of Popedoms on to the market.

Thus began the Second Great Schism of the Roman Catholic Church. It was the first really significant schism in the Church in over six hundred years and Edgar Malroy, who referred to it as the Great Cleavage, because it involved two massive tits, loved every minute of it.

?

The proof of design argument that I turned to next had a great deal of appeal, for it merely extrapolated the conditions I found myself in to the rest of the world. If the proof was correct, man was little more than a supermarket trolley in God's great and vaulted universe open twenty-four hours a day.

Was the proof of design argument the hidden rational foundation of my belief in God? I thought at first that it was. But climbing along what was known as the Geneva Spur I began to wonder, for was God the only possible logical explanation of non-human order in the world, as the proof argued?

Evolution could explain the order found in the living world without the need of a God of any kind.

Nor was it a mere toss-up between God and random chance.

David Hume, in his work *Dialogues Concerning Natural Religion*, first published three years after his death in 1779, had suggested, among other things, that the world might be a sort of giant cabbage and the order we perceive in it a product of this vegetable nature. He also suggested that the order we saw might easily be the work of more than one God-like figure, or perhaps the world was part of the web of a creature Hume called the Infinite Spider.

Edgar Malroy said once, in one of our heated discussions on God, that Hume had even suggested in the *Dialogues* that the universe was a complete pile of shit.

Hume had not actually said that, what he had said was: '*Why an orderly system may not be spun from the belly as well as from the brain, it will be difficult for him [the theologian] to give a satisfactory reason.*' *Dialogues*, Part VII.

Edgar Malroy said once that it was possible that the universe was shaped like a vagina.

There were, it seemed, an infinite number of possible explanations for the order in the world. To simply pick the explanation that employs a creator God seemed unreasonable, for why was that explanation, that hypothesis, more likely than any other?

Even if a creator God explanation was the only logically possible explanation of the order in the world, which it wasn't, it would be next to useless anyway, for what could it tell us about God? It was pretty impossible to tell very much at all about God looking at the shape the world was in. Certainly one could not conclude looking at a fossil of a fish that God wished us to worship on a Sunday or to cover our heads at all times or not kill cows or to pray five times a day or whatever.

Edgar Malroy told me, some time before I began climbing Everest, that it was possible to infer, looking around at God's supposed handiwork, that he was not good, in the normal sense of the word, and that he was not caring, in the normal sense of the word. Edgar then told me that there were only so many possibilities: either God was lazy or far less powerful then we thought, or he was equipped with a very sick sense of humour, or he was mad, or he was following some ridiculously alien moral system which we cannot, of course, comprehend. According to Edgar, any one of these possibilities was undesirable.

This had been roughly one of Edgar Malroy's arguments against the existence of God: there couldn't be a God because it would be so horribly sick if there was.

I went on pushing myself up Everest, my spiritual crisis getting worse with every passing day.

?

Another betting shop was opened just outside the walls of the Eastern Orthodox monastery of Mount Athos in Greece and thousands of Buddhist pilgrims in northern China queued up the face of Mount Wu Tai to place bets at the shop set up on the top of the sacred mountain.

On the 26th of September 2023 Scepticism Inc. distributed a total of two million tons of surplus food to the needy, opened new hospitals in Sierra Leone, Guinea, Afghanistan, Mali and Togo, paid for another six hundred eye operations, helped fund irrigation programmes in Morocco, Pakistan, Oman and Swaziland. It dropped another fifty prefabricated schools in remote parts of Lesotho, paid for the upkeep of tens of thousands of refugees, donated a total of thirty-three million pounds to major charities and immunised another thirty thousand children against the seven most common childhood diseases.

It was also on the 26th that Sophia Alderson made her appearance on the television programme *Today Talk*.

She talked about God and sin and looked as beautiful as all of George Milles Jr's wives put together.

She really did.

She said that nuclear power was safer than sex. She said that fossils were fake and that Darwin had been a fool. She said evolution was the dumbest thing she had ever heard of, with the possible exception of metaphysical betting.

44

When, a few days later, Edgar Malroy launched his 'Bet one get one free offer', profits soared ridiculously. By this time Scepticism Inc. had a betting shop in every major city and town in the UK and one in every state of America. There were betting shops outside every cathedral in Europe and just about every holy site you could think of. There were, for example, five betting shops in Lourdes alone.

Edgar Malroy, Scepticism Inc.'s Life Chairman, was everywhere at once. He was present when the King bet the Crown Jewels that he had a divine right to rule and he was present when the Archbishop of Canterbury made his three thousandth bet.

The archbishop had proved to be such a loyal and extravagant customer that after his three thousandth bet Edgar presented him with a gold medal made especially for him. It had a question mark on one side and a picture of a peanut on the other. The archbishop broke down when he received the medal. He said he was deeply touched. He looked deeply touched. He said thank you about a hundred times.

Edgar was also present when Ayatollah Khorasani bet £750,000 that Allah was Great.

Scepticism Inc. bought guns off the streets of the world's crime capitals for ten times their actual value and melted them down.

Scepticism Inc. paid ridiculous prices for peanut crops in areas formerly used to grow illegal drugs.

When war seemed about to break out anywhere in the world Edgar Malroy would fly in and literally buy the peace.

At least four invasions were prevented by Edgar Malroy in this way, as were an estimated twelve civil wars.

Leaders of countries, who for years had been hardly speaking, were seen on TV embracing each other, Edgar Malroy grinning behind them.

Free family planning clinics were opened in over two hundred countries with giant question marks hanging over the doorways and another four hundred fully functioning schools dropped out of the sky where they were needed most.

?

Sophia Alderson published a book called *Cosmic News Flash*. It was about six hundred pages long and was filled with references to the Bible, had hundreds of photographs of the Virgin Mary and several shots of the empty back seat of Sophia's old taxi cab. In the book, Sophia Alderson predicted that the end of the world was imminent, criticised world leaders for not following the teachings of the Bible, accused Pope John John of being too consumer-orientated and told the citizens of the world to humble themselves in the eyes of the Lord. She said UFOs and dinosaurs were the work of the Devil. She said the Bible was literally true and that Edgar had to be destroyed.

Two days before the release of *Cosmic News Flash* Sophia had informed her followers via loudspeaker and paper planes that placing bets at Metaphysical Betting Shops was an insult to the grace of God.

She made all of her followers promise not to place metaphysical bets ever again. Half of her followers couldn't bring themselves to make such a promise and left too upset to speak.

Those that remained removed their 'I've put my money where my metaphysics are' badges and jumped up and down on them, Sophia Alderson shouting into her loudspeaker:

'A-One-Two
A-One-Two
A-One-Two-Three-Four.'

When *Cosmic News Flash* was published one of the first people
to buy a copy was Edgar Malroy. He went home and underlined
with an HB pencil all the references to himself. There were well
over four hundred.

He was deeply touched.

Sophia Alderson was at the time the only religious leader in
the world to ban her followers from placing metaphysical bets.
Everyone else went on betting like mad.

In fact there were so many metaphysical bets being made by
this stage that Edgar had to start storing receipts on disused
oil platforms in the North Sea.

?

On the 11th of October Edgar called a press conference and said
that 'It would be funny if it wasn't so sad.' He was commenting
on the fact that he had become the wealthiest man ever.

45

At the same press conference Edgar said he proposed to triple
food production on the planet to end starvation.

He would do this by turning the deserts of the world into
high-yield farmland.

It would be the single most ambitious engineering project the
world had ever seen, would cost as estimated £100,000 billion
and would never be finished.

?

The Second Great Schism continued. St Peter's Square was divided in two by tape that said on both sides: 'Faithful do not cross.' The Metaphysical Betting Shop, situated in the middle, took bets from both sides.

Arguing violently with Pope John John's loyalists, Pope Philips and his rebels left Rome on the 13th of October 2023 along with his piano and flew to Rio de Janeiro where he set up his headquarters.

Pope Philips had very nearly missed the flight because he was busy writing out a cheque for £1.5 million on the bet that he was St Peter's successor.

The rumour in Rome at the time was that Pope Philips had sold a number of ancient manuscripts from the Vatican library to pay for this bet. Pope Philips' supporters denied this, saying that the funds had been made available by devoted followers.

Pope John John responded by betting three million pounds that *he* was St Peter's successor. Where Pope John John had got the money from was also a matter of some speculation.

'The Lord provides,' he told a reporter and tapped his nose.

Each Pope excommunicated the followers of the other on different TV channels at precisely the same time. Both warned that those people who followed the false Pope would burn in hell for ever and ever.

As a result of these two broadcasts Catholics ran screaming and shouting to Metaphysical Betting Shops all over the planet and endeavoured to outbet their rivals. Nest eggs, small, medium and large fortunes were spent at the Metaphysical Betting Shops, as if there was no tomorrow.

Soon each Pope was bragging about how much money his followers were betting. Edgar phoned the Popes with an update every three hours.

He called both Popes 'Your pompousness' and told them that

just possibly they were the biggest tits on the planet. Both Popes took such abuse stoically; they had to, they wanted to hear which of them was in the lead.

The antagonism got so bad between Pope John John and Pope Philips that each officially cursed, on live television, the followers of the other. Their cures were broadcast on the same channel, each Pope taking up half the screen.

They said some pretty terrible things.

This of course only exacerbated the matter further. Catholics became quite frantic, old women carried every last item they possessed to pawnbrokers so that they could put yet more money on the bet that their Pope was God's true messenger etc etc.

Normal betting shops were completely empty, bingo halls closed due to lack of custom and for the first time in living memory the Irish Grand National was called off because no one seemed very interested.

The queues outside the Metaphysical Betting Shops grew so large they blocked the traffic.

The queues outside the Metaphysical Betting Shops went on forever.

In just about every country there were reports of riots between rival Catholics. Armed supporters of one Pope guarded churches and cathedrals against attacks by supporters of the other Pope. Forty-five churches were burned down in suspicious circumstances. Eleven priests were beaten to death. There was even a reported case of someone being burned to death at the stake.

There was talk of a religious revival.

46

I went on climbing Everest, slowly.

It took over two years to get near to the summit. Seven hundred and thirty days of pushing through snow and over rocks searching for a proof of God that I never found. The traditional proofs were at best mere archaic hypotheses outdated and superseded. They were bad jokes, relying on felicitous logic and sophistry. They were childish delusions.

I cannot say how much despair I experienced when, near the summit of Everest, I finally saw that God's existence was utterly unprovable.

Everything else I believed, the time it took milk to go off at room temperature, or how many peanuts were consumed planet-wide in a year, or how to tell if a melon was ripe, I could provide evidence for, reasons why I believed them, but this was not so with my belief in God.

I tried rejecting it. I tried saying to myself that there was absolutely no evidence for God and that therefore it was illogical for me to believe in him.

But I couldn't do it. I couldn't stop believing. I believed as much in God then near the summit of Everest as I had done when Edgar wrote out the IOU for me more than two years before. I found myself entertaining both that there was no evidence for God at all and that I knew there was a God.

I thought I was going mad and of course I was.

?

It was lunchtime on the 2nd of August 2024. ShopALot was launching its Avocado Week, a promotional gimmick to remind its customers of the virtues of the smooth green Fuerte, the benefits of the Edrinol, the elegance of the Ryan and the seduction of the black Hass.

Pope John John and Pope Philips were still cursing each other like billy-o.

Sophia Alderson was being visited by the Virgin Mother in Rainthrope House. The Virgin Mother was wearing an old-fashioned diving suit and held a placard that said:

End of the World on Schedule

And I just sat there near the summit of Everest. Imagining Edgar Malroy saying to me in his irritating mid-Atlantic accent, 'I told you so, didn't I? You nut, I told you so.'

I was slipping slowly down the kaleidoscope-coloured furry slide of madness.

?

Edgar was particularly fond of the word nut. He used it all the time to describe his customers.

He did this partly, it seemed, because peanuts had been used by American missionaries in the late 1800s in their conversion efforts in China.

They gave each Chinaman who attended church a cupful of peanuts. They really did, Edgar had told me. 'The Chinamen sat through service after service absolutely captivated, they clapped and cheered, they loved it. Christianity caught on big time. Chinamen queued up for miles to hear the big funny foreigners tell them about their big funny God. All the new white churches were filled to bursting. Then the missionaries ran out of peanuts and there was not a single Chinaman to be seen.'

China was at one point the the largest producer of soya beans in the world.

114

47

'When is the world going to end?' boomed Sophia's beautiful voice.

'Really soon,' screamed back the two thousand followers outside the gates of Rainthrope House.

'Unless what?' boomed Sophia.

'Unless everyone listens to you, obeys God's will, repents and prays really, really hard,' shouted the crowd.

There wasn't a single 'I've put my money where my metaphysics are' badge to be seen. Edgar Malroy noticed this as his helicopter flew over the gates. It worried him a little.

Dr Cunningham, clipboard already in hand, was standing in the rain waiting for him.

As Edgar clambered out of the white helicopter and greeted the doctor he said, 'Lovely bow tie. Is it new?'

Dr Cunningham smiled just a little bit. Then he broke down.

Edgar did not stand behind the one-way mirror looking at Sophia Alderson, the love of his life, praying and making paper planes, for as long as he normally did. He was due to open a very special betting shop in a day or so and had to leave early.

Almost as soon as Edgar had slipped out of the observation room Dr Cunningham broke down. Again.

Sophia continued praying and making paper planes that told of the end of the world and a group of her followers erected a giant statue of the Virgin Mary outside the gates of Rainthrope House. The statue was at least eighteen feet tall and depicted the Virgin Mary in a beekeeper's outfit just as she had appeared to Sophia the night she informed her of the date for the end of the world.

As the statue was put in place followers of Sophia Alderson heard the news that Jane Cowen, the 92-year-old lady whose death Sophia had foretold, had passed away in the night.

Aloha.

The followers of Sophia Alderson got down on their hands and knees, praised the Lord, shouted hallelujah, called it a miracle, nodded like crazy and said told you so.

?

While I was suffering my spiritual crisis up Mount Everest, Scepticism Inc. opened its first drive-thru Metaphysical Betting Shop off the M1. The aim was to take a bet in under one minute. The first bet taken there was for £250,000 and was made by the Archbishop of Canterbury.

He and his wife had driven all the way from Lambeth Palace three nights before and spent every night in their car so that the archbishop could be the very first nut to use the drive-thru.

After the archbishop had placed his bet he was asked by reporters for his reaction to claims that his Church was dangerously short of cash. The archbishop said simply, 'I'm very pleased with the way things are going. Thank you.'

?

Pope John John and Pope Philips continued to insult each other and their followers. They sent hateful decrees to each other via fax. Around this time the Vatican released a new brand of bread called 'The Body of Christ'. ShopALot stores, like every other supermarket, sold the stuff.

Pope Philips said it was tasteless.

Pope John John said it was marketing.

The Schism was clearly causing horrendous damage to the Catholic Church. It had to be ended.

The only thing powerful enough to do this was a General Council, whose ruling would be binding on both Popes.

Attempts to call a General Council had begun as soon as the Schism had started. It was, however, only when Cardinal Morris of Westminster, who had throughout the early stages of the Second Great Schism kept an equal distance from both Popes, began calling for a General Council that it began to look even remotely possible.

Cardinal Morris visited both Popes and made literally thousands of phone calls to various members of the Church hierarchy. He pulled every string possible. He bribed. He threatened. He cajoled. He prayed.

Eventually a General Council was indeed summoned.

Catholics everywhere sighed in relief.

Things started nicely. Everyone was very polite to each other and called for unity. Things disintegrated into a shouting match and then something of a riot. Four Benedictine monks were seriously injured and Pope John John narrowly avoided a sixteenth-century chair thrown at him from across the room.

48

Another General Council was organised by Cardinal Morris only hours after the first one had collapsed. How he managed it no one ever found out. Pope Philips, flying back to Rio de Janeiro, had his plane return to Rome so that he could attend.

*   *   *

Things went much better at the second General Council; there was no fighting and the two rival Popes contented themselves merely making faces at each other. The second General Council met behind closed doors for four days.

Then a spokesman announced that the council had deposed both Popes for heresy.

An hour later Cardinal Morris was elected Pope. The first English Pope since Hadrian IV in 1150.

As news of this unforeseen development reached him Edgar Malroy laughed so hard that his false eye came out.

In fact he told me later he pissed himself with glee.

The three Popes denounced each other, then Pope Philips flew back to South America and Pope John John barricaded himself in his study with enough tins of food to last him till Judgement Day.

49

Just below the summit of Everest, I became convinced that George Milles Jr, the second wealthiest man ever and the inventor of the Infinity Chip, was waiting for me on the top of the tallest mountain in the world.

I started calling his name and shouting 'Aloha' as I reached the summit.

There was no response, of course.

Then I heard a noise almost undetectable. A whisper on the wind, a near nothing, hardly a sound at all, a memory of a sound, and it went like this:

50

A young man wanted to know the meaning of life. He was told that a wise old man, who lived on the top of a steep hill, knew the answer. The young man climbed the steep hill and asked the wise old man what the meaning of life was.

'Life', said the wise old man, 'is a fountain.'

'That's it? I climbed this steep hill for that?' said the young man, getting angry.

'OK,' said the wise old man. 'Life is not a fountain.'

Edgar Malroy

?

'Did someone say Aloha?'

There it was again.

I rushed upwards shouting, 'I did. I'm a supermarket trolley, I believe in the scientific method, the laws of gravity and commerce, I believe that any product with the word "new" on its packaging really is new. I believe in coupons, bulk-buying and for some quite unknown reason, which I simply cannot get my head around, I believe in God.'

I reached the top of a small rise and saw him. A short old man in a bright green ski jacket holding an oxygen mask in one hand and a satellite telephone in the other. He was waving at me.

I creaked over to him. I was on my last legs.

'George Milles Jr?' I said.

The old man took a good long intake of air from his oxygen mask then spoke. He said, 'My name isn't George Milles Jr.'

'It isn't?'

'It's Ronald Wooten, I'm a financial planning manager.'
'So where's God?'
'Who?' asked the man, putting his hand to his ear.
'God.' I said, getting desperate.
'Search me,' he said.

Somehow I pushed myself the last few metres to the summit. My Infinity Chip was all over the place. It couldn't take any more.

On the summit of Everest, almost hidden from view by a sea of flags, was a grey three-storey building. By the main entrance was a brass plaque which had the following words engraved on it:

The Himalayan Institute of Mountaineering

Next to the institute were two little shacks with the same word on each door:

Toilet

There were hundreds of people sitting in little groups. Some were talking on satellite phones, some were reading books, others were sleeping or writing postcards or preparing meals over camp stoves, some were relaxing in deckchairs listening to Walkmans.

There was a TV crew filming the little groups of people. Photographers were taking promotional shots of all manner of products propped up in the snow.

On another part of the summit three people were hastily putting together a hang-glider while a little further on five painters were busy in front of different sized canvases trying to catch the horizon that curved around them.

A few feet from the painters was a bunch of religious nuts. A Catholic priest, a Rabbi, three Muslims, a few Hindus, a Sikh, a liberal spread of Protestants and a number of Tibetan Buddhists. They were all arguing politely with each other about the nature of God and other stuff. Every few minutes or so they would all take deep inhalations of air from the oxygen masks they carried and look at their watches. Then the argument would start up again as if there had been no pause at all.

*   *   *

The painters asked them to keep their voices down, they were trying to concentrate.

There was then a great deal of commotion as a long procession of about forty figures marched onto the summit. They all wore white fur coats and were carrying tools, doors, desks, and pieces of wood.

'Thank God they're finally here!' shouted the Catholic priest as the religious nuts rushed to embrace the forty or so white figures.

'Erect it over here quick, hurry, hurry!' shouted the religious nuts, pointing at a patch of snow next to the Himalayan Institute of Mountaineering.

As the figures in the white fur overcoats headed for the spot, the religious nuts were jumping for joy, rasing their arms to heaven. Some were so excited they had forgotten to use their oxygen masks and their faces were turning light blue. Some nuts had faces almost the colour of blackberries.

It was then that I recognised Edgar Malroy limping amid the crowd, patting the religious men on their backs, laughing, telling them to calm down and saying things like, 'You really are quite nutty, you know that don't you?' His false eye was missing, his white fur overcoat was stained yellow around his crutch, and he was carrying a giant question mark over his shoulder as if it were a crucifix. He saw me, waved and said Aloha.

It was at this point, as Edgar and his employees set up the Metaphysical Betting Shop on the summit of Everest, that I went truly stark raving mad.

PART TWO

1

What happened was this:

I ruined three rather good attempts to capture the view from the summit of Everest on canvas. I gave three holy men concussion. I broke the giant question mark Edgar carried, turning it into a jagged exclamation mark. I uprooted four flags, I rammed the toilets and ran over, with my ravaged rubber wheels, dozens of the white clad Scepticism Inc. employees. I screamed, cried, and then fell over into a pile of snow, chewed chewing gum, used Popedoms, cigarette butts, empty beer cans and peanut shells.

Edgar and four others managed to carry me to the cable car that ran from the summit along the North-east Shoulder and then down the North Ridge. Scepticism Inc. had built the cable-car system for an estimated cost of £45 million.

When I had begun my attempt on Everest, the cable-car system was not even a spark in Edgar Malroy's eyes.

Halfway down the North Ridge of Everest I lost consciousness altogether.

?

I awoke in Edgar Malroy's office in Sceptic Tower. I knew it was Edgar's office because the altar he had used as his desk in the very first Metaphysical Betting Shop took up most of the room. Facing the altar/desk were two giant doors with question marks engraved on them. The three remaining walls were made of glass, as was the floor. It felt as if I was hovering 350 metres in the air above London.

On the altar/desk was a telephone, an HB pencil, a Geiger counter with no batteries in, a telescope, a computer terminal, a copy of *Cosmic News Flash*, a copy of the *Wall Street Journal* and a framed newspaper clipping of Sophia Alderson being put in a police van after her first attempt on Edgar's life.

Behind the altar/desk was a giant, almost three-dimensional, map of the world on which flashed thousands of tiny red lights, each one representing a Metaphysical Betting Shop. In the left-hand corner of the map near the tip of Canada were the words NUMBER OF BETS TAKEN and next to this, on dials rather like the scoreboards of old pinball machines, was a quite ridiculous number that rose steadily as I watched. Above Russia was a pound sign and another series of dials and an even more ridiculous number which also kept going up.

Above the map, embossed in gold, were the following words:

> *The folly of one man is the fortune of another*
> Francis Bacon

I watched the two ridiculous rows of numbers slowly rise for about ten minutes. Then they stopped.

On the glass walls of Edgar's office were framed receipts of metaphysical bets made by the world's spiritual leaders. There were the bets made by each of the three Popes, the bet made by the Dalai Lama, and the God is Great bet of Ayatollah Khotasani.

There were at least fifteen framed receipts belonging to the Archbishop of Canterbury.

I gazed out at the horizon, then the double doors opened outward and in limped Edgar and four pretty women in white swimsuits armed with improvised weapons. Edgar limped over to his desk and stared at the almost three-dimensional map. He looked old, his head was all bandaged up and his limp was worse than ever. 'Just as we feared, it's stopped. That must mean its planet-wide,' he said, tapping his three-dimensional map with his walking stick.

'When did it stop?'

'Just now,' I said.

'How are you feeling?' he asked, looking directly at me with his remaining eye.

'Different.'

'You had a Catastrophic System Degeneration, a sort of MBO but worse,' Edgar told me.

He then turned to one of the girls who was holding a box under her arm. She handed it to Edgar. 'This is for you,' he said and with a smile took out of the box a jar of peanut butter.

'The inventor of peanut butter, George W. Carrer of the Tuskegee Institute in Alabama, also invented peanut shampoo, peanut linoleum, peanut glue, peanut shoe polish, peanut shaving cream, peanut soap and even peanut axle grease,' I said.

Edgar opened the jar, inside of which was a photocopy of my bet that God existed. Wrapped in the receipt was a 1mm square of what looked like silicon.

'What is it?' I asked.

'Your belief in God. One of my technicians removed it this morning.'

'I don't believe you.'

'You also don't believe in God any more, do you? Have a go. Ask yourself.'

I didn't. The absolute certainty that the universe was under the watchful eye of an all-powerful being was completely and utterly gone. Poff. All that remained was a sort of fog.

'Well?' asked Edgar, putting down his Geiger counter. 'Is there a God?'

'Who knows?' I said.

At that Edgar and his four employees gave me a standing ovation and I realised I had become an agnostic.

2

After the standing ovation Edgar embraced me.

'Do you realise what this means?' he said. 'You couldn't help being a nut. It wasn't your fault, you weren't to blame. Isn't that wonderful? Isn't it the best news you ever heard? Doesn't it just make your day? There you were trying to prove something you thought you believed for a reason, racking your little brain, trying to be a good sensible supermarket trolley, when the whole thing was completely out of your hands. You've spent half your life trying to explain your blind faith in God, when it was just a silly little thing added to your Infinity Chip without your knowledge. And what did I, Edgar Malroy, do? I added insult to injury; what have I done incessantly from the moment our paths crossed? I have ridiculed and persecuted you for your silly belief in God. I called you nuts and laughed at you, I took your money just the same way I took all the real nuts' money.'

Edgar slithered to the floor in a heap. Two of the girls tried to help him up but he shooed them away.

'If only I had known! What a thing to do! What can I say? Oh the way I ridiculed you. "Oh look," I'd say, "the theist supermarket trolley" and "Here comes the trolley that believes in God." How could I? You've got to forgive me!'

Edgar was rolling around on the glass floor banging it with clenched fists.

'It's OK, Edgar,' I said. 'I understand.'

Immediately Edgar stopped seething around on the floor and looked up at me, surprised, relieved.

'Really? You're sure?' He slowly got to his feet and dusted down his cheap suit.

We took the lift first up to the top of the building and then all the way down to the main lobby on the ground floor. 'Its because of the shape, you see,' Edgar explained. I was in too dazed a state to realise what he was talking about.

The main lobby was like a battle zone. Dazed employees of Scepticism Inc. were sitting all over the place. Some jumped up when they saw Edgar limping purposefully towards them. Others were too exhausted to bother.

'Listen everyone!' he shouted, standing in the middle of the room, dusting his cheap suit down again. 'We have to search for survivors.'

I volunteered to come but Edgar thought it wasn't a good idea. He said people might think I was still nuts.

Edgar and about forty girls armed with all manner of improvised weapons left the lobby and the double doors were hastily shut behind them by employees too injured or exhausted or shocked to go.

'Will they be OK?' I asked.
'Who knows?' said the girl nearest me.

3

All over the planet electrical appliances had become homicidal maniacs. Just like that. One moment they were striving selflessly for the continued comfort of mankind, and the next they were threatening the very fabric of society.

They did horrible things. Things you can hardly imagine.

Alarm clocks bashed to death their sleeping owners. Stereos played so loudly they ruptured the eardrums of anyone within range. Heaters set fire to curtains. Dish-washing machines threw their contents like martial arts experts at anything that moved.

Electric shavers slit the throats of their users. Jacuzzis became death pits. Electronically controlled beds became torture racks. TVs exploded in the faces of their viewers. Lamps blew their bulbs with such force the effect resembled hand-grenade detonations, refrigerators entombed anyone unfortunate enough to get close, carving knives did some of their finest work, and blenders and food mixers did things too unspeakable to say.

Gas ovens exploded, laughing like crazy as they did so.

Prams committed infanticide.

Spin-dryers grabbed people's legs and gnawed them off. Irons worked on exposed flesh and toothbrushes committed mass murder.

It was hell.

Particularly in supermarkets.

They were death traps, the very worst places to be during the Great Mania. Check-out tills effectively barred the most natural escape routes while hordes of trolleys in a terrible frenzy ran over anyone they found.

Pope John John had the top half of his cranium removed by a Vatican electronic tin-opener. No one could come to his assistance because he had barricaded himself in his study. Just about everyone in the Vatican was said to have heard his screams.

When the Swiss Guards finally managed to force their way into the study the Pope was already dead.

It was the most horrific way in which a Pope had gone to heaven.

The electronic tin-opener managed to dispatch four middle-class Swiss Guards before it was finally destroyed. The tin-opener had gone through the guards' armour as if it wasn't there.

The sixteenth Dalai Lama was opening the very first ShopALot store in Tibet the moment the Great Mania took place. Everyone inside the store perished.

Millions of people fled built-up areas on foot, by car or on bicycle. It was the largest movement of people ever witnessed. Authorities declared states of emergency and martial law was imposed just about everywhere.

?

When Edgar and the others returned two hours later, they brought with them about twenty survivors.

When these survivors saw me, many of them started to scream and a few actually fainted.

After resting for about ten minutes, Edgar and the volunteers went out in search of more survivors. They did this in all four times that night and it was a very brave thing to do.

Back in Edgar's office the ridiculous figure over Canada remained frozen at:

3346,627,201

4

The lobby of Sceptic Tower became a sort of hospital. Edgar and his employees ran the place as best they could with first-aid kits.

It was about nine o'clock in the evening when we heard the distant rumble. It sounded just like the avalanches on Everest.

Edgar slowly pushed the main doors open as the noise grew. It was coming from London Bridge. It was a roar now, deafening.

Edgar, standing in the doorway, put his hands over his ears.

The crowd appeared from around the corner of King William Street. A fat dirty oily snake of humanity, filling the whole road from pavement to pavement, spilling down alleyways and back streets, lapping against shop windows. A lump of heads, arms and feet moving frantically forward.

Here and there a figure would topple over, pushed down by those behind, and disappear from view, washed over by countless legs.

The screeching crowd, now filling the whole of King William Street and beyond, steamed onwards at an alarming rate.

Dogs barked furiously. Children, some laughing, some crying, detached themselves from the crowd and then joined it again.

The mass of people were very excited about something. They were nodding furiously, pointing at every sign of destruction around them, and they were heading straight towards us.

The giant doors to Sceptic Tower were slowly closed. Edgar just stood there looking at the oncoming mass of people. His hands were no longer covering his ears.

Just before the doors were closed it was possible to see that many in the crowd were carrying illegible placards. Just before the doors were slammed shut both Edgar and I saw Sophia Alderson at the head of the frantic mass being pushed in a wheelbarrow by Dr Cunningham. In another wheelbarrow being pushed by a follower of Sophia was the loudspeaker system from Rainthrope House.

Sophia was sitting in her wheelbarrow, as beautiful as the Tarantula Nebula seen in infra-red.

The shouts and screams from outside grew louder.

The loudspeaker system was turned on.

There was terrible feedback at first. Then the sweetest voice you ever heard echoed through the door and filled the main lobby and reverberated throughout the ten million square feet of office space that made up Sceptic Tower.

'Well, I told you so, didn't I? I warned you this was going to happen, I folded paper planes with the Truth written on them. I tried to save everyone from themselves. I tried to prevent this. A righteous few heeded my words and saw the light, but the great mass of ignorant blind humanity went on using microwaves on Sundays, went on betting on religion. You had to go on browning pieces of bread and wearing odd socks and being all liberal didn't you? You had to go on picking your noses with gay abandon as if it would have no consequence at all. Well, do you see now? Do you finally see? Make no mistake, the destruction and death all around us is God's glorious work and what's more we deserve it. We deserve every last bit. Your aunt got roasted to death on her friendly sunbed? She was asking for it. Your brother got hacked to little pieces by the Flymo? He had it coming. They all had it coming. They didn't believe enough. They didn't listen to me.'

There were moans from outside as the followers of Sophia, nodding in agreement, got down on their hands and knees and prayed to God for all they were worth.

Sophia, with her angelic voice, continued:

'Edgar Malroy, you spawn of Satan, you who are evil incarnate, a creature from the deepest pit of hell, we know you are in this blasphemous place with your skimpily clad sacrilegious harlots. We have come to hear you renounce your sins for the sake of the world, for the little children, Edgar. Come out from that den of iniquity this instant.'

The crowd of nuts began erecting a massive bonfire, using anything they could lay their shaking hands on: doors, benches, chairs from nearby offices, everything that would burn. They were hopping mad, delirious and nodding so ferociously by this stage I was sure their heads would fall right off.

Sophia shouted into her loudspeaker system some more about

how she had known this was going to happen and how Edgar Malroy had to submit to the glory of God.

It was then, as the nuts were putting the finishing touches to their bonfire, that Edgar Malroy made a very serious error of judgement.

This is what he did: before I or anyone else could stop him he pushed open the giant doors and limped out, waving with his good hand for the crowd of foaming, screeching nuts to quieten down.

Which they did only because they had not expected Edgar Malroy to have given up so easily. They were dumbstruck. It was almost disappointing for them.

There was this odd silence. Everyone wanted to hear what Edgar Malroy was going to say. He said this:

'Assorted nuts, I have an announcement to make. Am I to assume that you believe the terrible events that have befallen us all recently to be the handiwork of God, forced to act by our sinful behaviour and our failure to repent?'

Sophia, Dr Cunningham and the rest of the numberless followers nodded as one, and I was yet again afraid that all their heads would topple off.

'I see. Well, unfortunately, due to the very crisis in question, I am unable to take any metaphysical bets at this time. Sorry. So keep your money, go home to your families, tidy things up and come again when this terrible calamity has passed. OK? Thank you very much for your attention. Thank you again and good night.'

Edgar bowed and the crowd proceeded to hurl all manner of projectiles at him, bricks, bits of concrete, and parts of smashed-up former conscious electrical appliances.

Without really thinking, I rushed out of Sceptic Tower and placed myself in front of Edgar, shielding him from the assortment of missiles. Sophia fired at Edgar from her wheelbarrow with an old

Chinese assault rifle modelled on the Soviet AK47 and used for a time by East Timor resistance fighters in their struggle with Indonesia. Where she got it from no one ever found out. The bullets ricocheted off my metal frame.

The crowd, worked into a terrible rage by the sound of gunfire, and the sheer effrontery of Edgar, charged forward. Edgar crawled inside the main lobby, the doors closing swiftly behind him due to the crush of screaming madmen that had slammed up against them. I was smothered, grappled, hoisted over the seething mass of gibbering lunatics and given a close-up view of their placards, which seemed to have written on them things like:

> The crakled reome on!

and

> Erra broob am!

I was carried this way and that above the ocean of metaphysicians. At first I thought my direction was purely random, but then I realised where I was heading; they were carrying me towards the bonfire.

5

I was rather unceremoniously tossed onto the top of the bonfire and it was quickly set alight.

Time passed. The rubber of my wheels began to melt.

The flames inched upwards through the stack of office furniture.

The throng of nuts danced around the blaze, shaking their fists at me, accusing me of being a bedfellow of the Devil or something. Sophia Alderson kept telling me to repent. She was so beautiful that I would have done readily if I knew what the hell she was talking about.

More time passed. My frame began to warp something terrible.

My push-bar drooped.

Then there was a terrible wooshing noise as a white helicopter with question marks on its doors descended from the sky directly above me. The flames flattened out and I felt two pairs of hands grab my push-bar and then I heard someone yell, 'Up!' and then the fire was spiralling away beneath me.

I was smoking like a burnt marshmallow.

I was pulled inside the helicopter by a brunette and a redhead who were both wearing heatproof gloves. In the front seat next to the pilot was Edgar Malroy, who was blowing kisses to Sophia Alderson. He really was.

She pretended not to notice.

We landed on the top of Sceptic Tower. The rubber of my wheels had melted right off. All that remained of them were four little grey pools on the floor of the helicopter.
    That was not all. Edgar pointed it out first. He said, 'I don't know how to tell you this, but ... well, you're sort of curved.'

This was really an understatement. I was bent like a banana.

We stayed up on the roof of the Sceptic Tower until I had cooled down and stopped smoking.

Then I was manhandled back to Edgar's transparent office.

Once there Edgar grabbed the telescope on his desk and put it to his false eye, then he placed it over his working eye and told us what he saw.

He could barely make out Sophia in her wheelbarrow. He could, however, clearly see the giant white statue of the Virgin Mary wearing a beekeeper's outfit being brought towards the tower by hundreds of nuts.

'They're going to ram us!' he screamed, dropping the telescope. He began making his way frantically to the main lobby. The two employees of Scepticism Inc. picked me up and raced after him.

We reached the lobby as Sophia's followers rammed the doors with the giant statute of Mary for the thirtieth time. The doors were giving. They bowed horribly with each ram. We could hear the crowd outside screaming and nodding like mad. 'The next one. The next one will do it!' they shouted.

Edgar got whiter with each thud. 'Physical death is most likely the end. The idea of a soul, an immaterial thing that survives death, like all religious dogma is nothing more than a pathetic, antiquated guess masquerading as a fact,' he said to no one in particular.

There was another ram, the door bowed horribly again and Edgar went whiter.

'Belief in a soul is perhaps the ultimate in wishful thinking. It is the final expression of the conceited belief that I am too important to die.'

There was another ram. People inside the tower were screaming, running everywhere looking for somewhere to hide. Edgar just stood there mumbling on about the non-existence of the soul. I would have looked for a place to hide like any sane person but my wheels had been burned off and because I was all bent, on my own I could only move in a tight circle. The two girls who carried me from the roof had disappeared.

'The fifth-century Chinese philosopher Fan Chen said that

"The soul is to the body what sharpness is to the knife." We have never known the existence of sharpness after the destruction of the knife. How can we admit the survival of the spirit when the body is gone?'

'I don't know, Edgar, but shouldn't we hide like everyone else?' I said, going around and around the short, slightly over-weight man.

'Huh? Oh there's little point, they'll find us. Anyway a man, or supermarket trolley, who rejects the idea of the soul will have greater respect for conscious life,' said Edgar, who was by this stage very white.

On the thirty-third ram a hairline fracture appeared running the length of the statue from the top of the hood to the tip of the sandal that protruded, some felt scandalously, from under the gown. No one saw the fracture.

'You know, to be perfectly honest, I'm surprised all this lasted as long as it did. It was a sort of joke really,' said Edgar, taking hold of my push-bar with both hands and turning me to face the crowd that we expected would at any second come screaming through the mangled remains of the door.

'Aloha,' I said.

'Aloha,' said a very very white Edgar Malroy.

On the thirty-fourth ram the statute shattered and fell to the ground in a million pieces.

?

Time passed.

The nuts just stood there outside the tower.

Then they threw themselves at the door. They tried everything. Sophia ordered Dr Cunningham to charge at the door with her

138

and her wheelbarrow. He did so three times before Sophia got a headache and ordered him to stop.

After that everyone sort of milled about for about an hour, praying and chanting, not really sure what to do with themselves. Then Sophia ordered Dr Cunningham to turn her wheelbarrow around and she and her followers headed back over London Bridge to the Kingdom of God, the new name they had given Rainthrope House.

When the last nut had marched begrudgingly away, Edgar fainted and slumped over me.

I, too, eventually fell asleep.

I dreamt of supermarkets.

No one opened the doors until morning. Then, as most of us slept, someone swept the million bits of broken statue into a pile. The only recognisable thing left of the Madonna were her praying hands. Someone, probably the same person who had swept the bits up, placed the hands on the top of the pile of rubble, and when Edgar woke up desperate for a pee at about ten o'clock he called it art.

I got better. Sort of.

My wheels were replaced but I remained as bent as a banana.

6

Half an hour after Edgar remarked on the rubble, a column of trucks, light tanks and jeeps reached Sceptic Tower.

All day soldiers engaged in vicious house-to-house fighting with diehard toasters, kettles, washing machines etc etc. We could hear the sound of gunfire and hand-grenade detonations all around the tower. Where resistance was particularly stiff, buildings would be strafed by attack helicopters or shelled by artillery batteries set up in car parks and open spaces three or four kilometres away. If that failed to do the trick whole streets were flattened by 1000-pound high explosive bombs dropped by fighter bombers.

The same sort of military operations were going on all over the world, as humans fought to reclaim their towns and cities.

Edgar and I watched the fighting from his office. Little columns of smoke ascended from windows where soldiers dispatched electronic appliances.

The wounded we had looked after were evacuated by army ambulance to Hyde Park, where a massive emergency aid camp had been set up. Policemen, all heavily armed, arrived by the afternoon. Four of them sat outside Sceptic Tower on the rubble that had once been the statue of the Virgin Mary and talked and told jokes.

More truckloads of soldiers drove past Sceptic Tower all evening as did dump trucks which were used to collect the mutilated bodies that were all over the place.

By mid morning of the next day the dump trucks and the soldiers had gone. Only police and weeping insurance men could be seen on the streets.

It was then that Edgar and I heard an almost imperceptible sound, the sound of the dials above Edgar's almost three-dimensional map of the world starting to turn.

Betting in the countless Metaphysical Betting Shops around the world had started up again and slowly things began to return to something approaching normality.

?

Sophia began talking of God giving humanity one final chance and, unobserved by anyone, apart from Dr Cunningham behind the one-way mirror, shunted the red marker that represented the end of the world along her wall chart a little.

?

Over fifty million people had been killed, nearly as many as had died in the Second World War.

?

It was agreed by just about everyone that the belief in God built into the Infinity Chip had been the cause of the Great Mania and they redoubled their attempts to trace Thomas Duncombe, who had gone into hiding since the Ding Dong 7 incident. No one knew where he was.

The L. Beno corporation was promptly sued by just about everyone on the planet, for murder and for post-traumatic stress disorder, and the largest transnational in the world was declared bankrupt in a very short space of time. The stock market crashed as it had done when George Milles Jr had passed away.

Leonard Duncombe, the owner of the L. Beno corporation and Thomas Duncombe's father, publicly disowned his son. Again. Leonard Duncombe then went back to his ancestral home in Venice and wrote a short treatise on why God cannot exist because there is so much stupidity and religion in the world. After writing this treatise Leonard Duncombe committed suicide by slitting his wrists with the broken head of the porcelain cat he had been buying when he had bumped into the woman who became his wife. The porcelain cat was the conversation piece by which the two became acquainted.

Aloha.

Leonard Duncombe's collection of porcelain cats, the second largest such collection in the northern hemisphere and valued at £1.5 million, was smashed to smithereens by grief-stricken Italians.

Everyone said that George Milles Jr was turning in his grave and of course he was.

Every single chain of supermarkets went to the wall. People couldn't bring themselves to enter such places. It brought back too much pain.

?

I was the only conscious supermarket trolley left alive on the planet. In fact I was the only conscious electrical appliance left alive on the planet.

Edgar kept me hidden away on the higher floors of Sceptic Tower where he and only his most trusted staff ever saw me. I owe Edgar Malroy my life – there is little doubt of that.

?

In addition to Thomas Duncombe and the Jehovah's Witnesses, some people blamed George Milles Jr for inventing the Infinity Chip in the first place; just how, still no one knew. An electromagnetic transmission, broadcast on the same wavelength as this one, was sent out into space from the world's largest radio telescope, the Arecibo, in Puerto Rico, in roughly the same direction as the transmission sent out six years earlier during George Milles Jr's lavish funeral service. It went as follows:

> *George Milles Jr invented the Infinity Chip.*
> *Six years later and fifty million people are dead.*
> *We just thought you ought to know.*

Other people blamed the weather.

7

Naturally enough the Jehovah's Witnesses were persecuted terribly all over the world and outlawed in France and Canada. Again. Just about every single Kingdom Hall was ransacked and the religion or cult very nearly died out altogether.

Every single former Kingdom Hall, roughly thirteen thousand buildings around the world, was bought by Edgar and turned into a Metaphysical Betting Shop.

The only difference between a cult and a religion, according to Edgar Malroy, is the number of nuts who subscribe to the nonsense peddled. If there are just a few nuts then it is a cult, if there are lots of nuts then it is a religion.

Everyone agreed that it had been a good thing that the Jehovah's Witnesses had decided against building a third mansion to house the prophets in when they returned to Earth, because very likely it would have been blown sky high after the Great Mania.

The few Jehovah's Witnesses left had to not celebrate Christmas all year round in secret. They also told only their closest friends of their belief that only 144,000 true believers would go to heaven and that Jesus had died on a stake and not a cross.

Sophia Alderson blamed everyone who hadn't listened to her for the Great Mania. Her following mushroomed out of all proportion and great swathes of people stopped eating toast. The planet-wide consumption of carrot juice rose by thirty per cent. Sheep and a few cows in Devon were even seen wearing jumpers and woollen shorts, and Rainthrope House, which had long ago ceased to be any kind of medical institution, became swamped by thousands and thousands of followers.

The only member of staff who remained was, of course, Dr Cunningham, in what capacity, no one, including himself, really knew.

Edgar blamed nuts in general and 'this God idea', the childish habit humans had of ascribing onto the world human-like qualities like caring and purpose. 'The world doesn't care!' he would shout sometimes, looking through his telescope at the rebuilding of London after the Great Mania. 'It just doesn't care.'

Who do I blame? I blame providence.

If it had, that is, only been a cooler day perhaps Thomas Duncombe wouldn't have had a drink, wouldn't have got his hand stuck, and wouldn't have been freed by two soaking wet Jehovah's Witnesses. But I am blaming the weather, a very nutty thing to do – and I have tried, since obtaining, 79,999 years ago, my diploma in agnosticism, to keep to a minimum the nutty things I do.

I try.

?

Following the death of the sixteenth Dalai Lama over fifteen thousand bets were made on the matter of his reincarnation.

The Panchen Lama, whose role it was historically to find the Dalai Lama's reincarnation, left the Tashilhunpo Monastery with some thirty monks on Japanese superbikes. Hundreds of journalists and a mobile betting shop, which had in a former life been an ice-cream van, followed the Panchen Lama.

?

The Panchen Lama, the monks, the press and the mobile betting shop travelled some twenty-five miles to a place known as the Shugtri Ridge, which overlooked Lhamo Latso, the Vision Lake.

The Panchen Lama and the monks sat on the Shugtri Ridge and chanted the mystic syllable Om and other sacred words amid a forest of prayer flags.

When the submarine on the back of an articulated lorry reached the ridge, the Panchen Lama climbed inside and the monks got to work lowering the vessel into the Vision Lake.

8

The Panchen Lama remained submerged under the Vision Lake in the submarine for nearly four days. The monks on the Shugtri Ridge above prayed like billy-o.

Bubbles could be seen rising from the deep and newsmen and women reported from the lake's edge.

Speculation among the monks was rife.

The mobile betting shop ran out of badges.

In time for the evening news slot in most European countries the Panchen Lama surfaced. The submarine was quickly winched back up to the Shugtri Ridge. There the Panchen Lama told reporters that he had seen something deep in the Vision Lake. Exactly what the Panchen Lama wouldn't say.

Whatever he had seen led the Panchen Lama, his monks, the world's press and a hastily restocked mobile Metaphysical Betting Shop to a remote mountainside village and the home of a Sherpa, whose baby son had been born at the precise moment the Dalai Lama had opened the supermarket.

The boy, whose strangely European-sounding name was Andrew Pinchbeck, underwent a battery of mystical tests, all of which he passed.

For example, he correctly identified personal items of the former Dalai Lama such as an empty tube of toothpaste and a half-finished bottle of Scotch.

There was jubilation at this and the mobile Metaphysical Betting Shop ran out of badges. Again.

The child was even said to have the old Dalai Lama's grin.

He was taken by the Panchen Lama to the Tashilhunpo Monastery and, following an elaborate and deeply touching ceremony, became the seventeenth Dalai Lama.

Immediately after the ceremony the Panchen Lama flew to London and bet £100,000 that Andrew Pinchbeck was indeed the reincarnation of the sixteenth Dalai Lama.

It was then that Scepticism Inc. staff turning the former ShopALot store in Tibet into a betting shop found the sixteenth Dalai Lama alive and well in the frozen meat section.

What had happened was this:

The sixteenth Dalai Lama, seeing all the mayhem and slaughter around him, had leapt into one of the freezer units and put himself into a trance. The combined effect of his trance and the temperature of the freezer meant that the sixteenth Dalai Lama achieved a sort of suspended animation.

When the sixteenth Dalai Lama was told about the finding of the seventeenth Dalai Lama he very nearly went into another trance.

Tibetan Buddhists sided either with the old Dalai Lama or the new and, needless to say, Edgar Malroy made a killing.

?

The Great Mania, the single most bloody event in the history of the human race, had not helped settle the Second Great Schism of the Roman Catholic Church. Both the remaining Popes blamed the other and the late Pope John John for the tragedy.

When Pope John John's death had been announced his followers solemnly queued up outside Metaphysical Betting Shops and spent ridiculous sums of money betting that his holiness had gone straight to heaven. The rival Pope's followers queued up and spent an equal amount of money betting that Pope John John had gone to hell.

Who knows?

A new Pope was hastily elected from the cardinals who had been loyal to Pope John John and an estimated 3.3 million Catholics headed back to the betting shops to show just how much they believed Pope Ingram's election was the will of God.

Edgar made an estimated ten million pounds the evening Cardinal Ingram was declared Pope.

Excommunications and curses followed as a matter of course and Popedom production was increased by twenty-five per cent.

9

A week after the Great Mania, Scepticism Inc. opened another five thousand betting shops all over the place. Every single one of the new betting shops had formerly been a supermarket.

Scepticism Inc. profits rose incredibly, unbelievably. If anything, more people were making metaphysical bets than had done so before the Great Mania. The number of MBO cases grew, as did the number of nuts attending the weekly sessions of Metaphysical Betting Anonymous.

Polls showed that eighty-five per cent of the population of the UK had placed at least one metaphysical bet. Twenty-five per cent had placed so many bets they had actually lost count.

One of those who had lost count was the Archbishop of Canterbury. In fact he had lost count of how many times he had lost count. He was a very devout man. He seemed to spend almost all of his time betting. Many of his fellow priests in the Anglican Church were equally bitten by the metaphysical betting bug; some even went as far as to close their churches on Sundays while they handed out vast sums of money to pretty women in white swimsuits with furry pink question marks that bobbed to and fro on their heads.

?

Scepticism Inc. began again in various ways to create the least pain and the longest life for as many as possible. Scepticism Inc. dropped another five hundred prefabricated schools, distributed incredibly effective fertilizer for nothing to low-income farmers, handed out over ten million tonnes of cereal to families in Zambia, Angola, Tanzania, Ruanda, Uganda, Singapore and the Philippines.

Scepticism Inc. funded irrigation projects in the river basins of the Niger, Brahmaputra, the Ganges and the Mekong, for an estimated cost of fifty billion pounds. Edgar's company gave out supplies of vitamins to third world countries and set up twenty-five agricultural research institutes in various parts of the world to look into ways of improving local food crops and farming techniques.

Edgar during this time talked incessantly about how he would turn the world's largest deserts into farmland. He was sure this would triple the Earth's food production and thus end starvation.

Optimism, Edgar would say, is not knowing what isn't possible.

In this particular case Edgar was wrong about what wasn't possible. The deserts of the world would remain deserts and people would go on starving in horrible unimaginable numbers.

10

Pope Ingram increased Popedom production by another twenty-five per cent to coincide with the launch of a massive advertising campaign. The campaign's slogan was this:

Only a *real* Catholic would use one.

At the same time the boys in the Vatican brought a new product on to the market in an attempt to recoup some of the massive losses they had sustained as a result of the demise of the supermarkets.

The new product was called Popegum, a very dry and rather bland chewing-gum which came in packets with the image of a crucified Jesus Christ printed on them.

Pope Ingram declared at a press conference that the action of chewing Popegum not only exercised the muscles of the jaw and thus relieved facial tension, it brought one closer to God. It also, he insisted, wouldn't spoil one's appetite.

Supporters of Pope Ingram began chewing like crazy and £100,000 was spent on a metaphysical bet supporting the mystical nature of Popegum.

Chewing-gum consumption quadrupled to thirty million pounds a year.

Popegum was sold in churches and cathedrals. Almost all the proceeds went to fund the Pope's metaphysical claim to be the one and only messenger of God.

Pope Philips and Pope Morris declared that any Catholic who chewed Popegum was instantly excommunicated. Things got to be so bad that any Catholic who was seen chewing any sort of gum at all was frowned on heavily by both Pope Philips and Pope Morris' followers.

Whether a Catholic chewed or not became a good indicator of his allegiance, and in countries all over the world fights broke out when chewing Catholics encountered non-chewing Catholics.

Some Catholics who backed Pope Philips went so far as to only eat food which did not need to be chewed, such as jelly, pasta and soup.

Pro-Ingram Catholics called such devoutly loyal supporters of Pope Philips, suckers.

While the disagreement over Popegum worsened, there were rumours that every one of the three Popes had taken out massive loans from various banks in order to fund their metaphysical claims.

Every Pope denied they were in any sort of financial difficulty but the fact remained that it was a particularly expensive business to declare oneself Pope.

?

It was while I was hidden away in the upper levels of Sceptic Tower that Edgar Malroy taught me the Errr.

A true agnostic, he said, had to constantly purge his mind of metaphysical beliefs, had to practise balancing on the fence. 'The fence has much better views, and is very wide. In fact there is a nice Italian restaurant and a heated swimming pool on the fence and there is no reason to ever come down,' Edgar told me smiling.

Errring was one way of staying on the fence. A fence balancer had to flush out all that metaphysical crap, all the wild guesses pretending to be facts, they had been exposed to.

Edgar said that everyone should Errr at least once a week, particularly on Sundays.

Errring, Edgar said, was the mental equivalent of going to the toilet.

'The thing to remember is this; we simply cannot know metaphysical truths, but this doesn't, when you think about it, matter all that much.

'So we don't know the supreme meaning to everything; at least we know that we don't know. It's a damn silly sort of question anyway really. I mean absolute truth, who needs it? It is simply something we can learn to live without. Our glorious ignorance of all things metaphysical, absolute truth, and all that crap doesn't have to inhibit us at all. In fact it can free us. As the great sceptic Pyrrho observed, no longer asking the question is almost the same thing as getting the right answer,' said Edgar and then he showed me how to Errr.

This is how to Errr:

Think of some metaphysical claim, something some nut might bet on, say for example that God is always good. Examine this claim carefully and take a deep breath. Next consider another metaphysical claim which is the complete antithesis of the first claim; for example, God is always bad. Examine this claim carefully and take another deep breath.

Now think about the first claim again and this time raise your right leg in the air. (In my case I tilted myself to the right.) Lower your right leg and then think about the second claim and as you do so raise your left leg. Do this over and over, increasing the speed with which you move from your right foot to your left foot and make the noise 'Errrrrrr'.

The trick is to try to step from one foot to the other so fast that you seem to think both mutually exclusive metaphysical propositions at the same time.

Some members of staff at Scepticism Inc. claimed to have reached the state where they were entertaining both claims, but Edgar himself confessed he had never managed it.

I was never that good at Errring while on Earth. When I left the funny little planet I spent most of my time Errring. There was not much else to do and travelling through space there is a great danger one will start to have all-sorts of metaphysical ideas.

I have performed Errring millions of times now and like Edgar I have never quite managed to hold two mutually exclusive metaphysical propositions at the same time. Maybe, one day, as I wait here, I will.

Who knows?

After Edgar had shown me the basics of Errring he pushed me out of his office saying I should try it on my own and picked up the phone and spoke with the President of Egypt.

11

People hung on Sophia Alderson's every beautiful word. Her vague predictions and warnings, often accompanied by graphic illustrations, were printed in newspapers around the world above the horoscope sections and her picture appeared in just about every magazine on the planet.

Sophia was interviewed literally thousands of times. She appeared on chat shows demanding everyone repent and so on. Hundreds of articles were written about how she interpreted the Bible (correctly, of course, she claimed) and how she did her hair. Her wardrobe was examined almost as much as her theology. Sophia Alderson published recipes that showed proper respect for God and books showing how to knit clothes for all of God's creatures including moths and greenfly.

Of course thousands more fell in love with her, unable to help themselves.

She was so beautiful it was silly.

Sophia's loudspeaker system was improved and TV screens projected massive images of her angelic face to the thousands and thousands of followers who had started camping out in the grounds of Rainthrope House.

Lookalikes started appearing all over the place, which only made Edgar miss even more his visits to Rainthrope House, which had ceased after the Great Mania. He pined for Sophia something awful. He bought every magazine she appeared in, underlining with his HB pencil any attack she made against him, and she made many such attacks. He would watch over and over again videos of her chat show appearances, memorise the interviewers' questions so that it would seem that he and she were having a conversation. He stared out at the horizon from his office, paced up and down and sighed a lot.

?

Although busy planning for the end of starvation by transforming the world's deserts into farmland and expanding his massive metaphysical betting empire, Sophia Alderson was never really far from Edgar's troubled mind. Sometimes he'd order all of his employees out of his office, just sit there twiddling with his Geiger counter that didn't have any batteries in and probably never would, and think of the beautiful nut.

He even said her name in his sleep and played with himself

thinking about her in his question-mark-shaped bathtub on the 145th floor of Sceptic Tower.

Edgar told me over and over again about how he had met Sophia for the first time. I kept reminding him that I had been there but he kept on telling me anyway.

'She wouldn't leave until I agreed to shut down the Metaphysical Betting Shop and I told her I'd never dream of doing such a thing.'

Edgar would go on to tell me how Sophia had called him a smartarse, a smug little nitwit, a sinner, a spawn of Satan among other things and how he had called Sophia a nut, of course, a silly little girl who had never grown up, an irrational bitch and so on. Edgar would then gaze out at the horizon. In Edgar's office in Sceptic Tower it was rather hard not to gaze out at the horizon.

He told me how the two of them had argued outside on the grass and how a pigeon had shat in Sophia's golden hair as she was arguing that everything that happened, happened with a purpose.

He told me with tears in his remaining eye how, after Sophia had got most of the pigeon shit out of her golden hair, he had said that he was sceptical about the purpose people had in saying there was a purpose to life. He smiled fondly, remembering what had happened next; how tenderly, as if sharing a special secret, he had slowly pulled down his trousers to reveal among other things his and Nietzsche's view on life having a purpose.

He told me that after that he and Sophia had not spoken to each other for two months. 'It was like putting everything you ever owned in twelve massive tea chests, carrying them on to an ocean liner and then standing on the dockside as the ship set sail for Papua New Guinea.'

I told Edgar I knew what he meant.

Edgar then asked if I thought it was possible to disagree with someone violently, absolutely, to consider them immoral and nuts and yet still love them.

I told Edgar I thought it was a long shot.

Then he started asking me what I thought Sophia was doing at that very moment. I told him she was more then likely praying. He agreed.

'I love that woman, you know,' he said after a little pause.

'But Edgar,' I said, 'she's tried to kill you on two separate occasions.'

Edgar smiled and looked off at the horizon, then looked at me as if I was taking everything far too seriously and said:

'Well, yes, a bit.'

12

After a series of delicate telephone negotiations the sixteenth Dalai Lama flew to the Tashilhunpo Monastery to try and sort things out.

The sixteenth Dalai Lama said to reporters before going inside, 'We are all Buddhists here, a solution will be found without excessive violence, wait and see.'

The sixteenth Dalai Lama then posed holding the seventeenth Dalai Lama in his arms and kissed the baby's waxy forehead a number of times. Everyone agreed they had the same grin. 'See, there are no hard feelings here. We love each other. See, I treat him as if he were myself,' said the older Dalai Lama. The seventeenth Dalai Lama started to cry. 'See,' said the sixteenth Dalai Lama, 'he already knows that life is suffering.'

?

A dozen of Sophia's most nutty followers began sitting around her bed listening to her snoring in the vain hope that she would utter something interesting in her sleep.

Dr Cunningham sat at the énd of her bed every night with his clipboard. He told the other followers crowding the room that the clipboard was to write down whatever God's messenger might utter in her sleep.

In fact Dr Cunningham ticked the clipboard every time Sophia breathed and her angelic, perfect bosom rose under her white sheets and an erection uncreased his trousers.

?

Sophia remained the only religious leader in the world to ban her followers from using Edgar Malroy's services. She said betting was worse than murder – maybe it was.

Who knows?

The other religious leaders didn't understand what all the fuss was about. Many thought Sophia was a little nutty themselves.

Not only in Sophia's eyes was metaphysical betting a most heinous crime, but standing by while people placed bets on religion and philosophy was almost as bad. She broke down whenever she spoke of the millions of people who foolishly put money on their metaphysical beliefs. She called the millions of people taken in by Edgar the 'lost ones'.

To save the 'lost ones' Sophia organised pickets outside Metaphysical Betting Shops. These pickets normally consisted of five or six nuts who held illegible placards and tried to turn away the multitude of people who, at just about any time of day, would be queuing to place bets on things they couldn't prove. Hardly any of the 'lost ones' listened to the followers of Sophia and no one could make out what their placards were supposed to say.

Sometimes Sophia's followers, nodding and crying with despair, would try saving the 'lost ones'' souls by physically preventing them from placing bets. They would tie them to lamp-posts with rope.

When Sophia's followers trapped metaphysicians in this way, the managers of the betting shops would phone the police and eventually the metaphysicians would be released, more determined than ever to exchange their money for a silly receipt and an even dumber badge.

?

Negotiations between the three Lamas went on and on. It reminded the sixteenth Dalai Lama of the time he had been a South African miner who had spent four gruelling days trapped in a lift shaft thirty kilometers from Bitterfontein.

He had eventually died in the mine when his air pocket ran out. Aloha.

On the balcony of the Tashilhunpo Monastery the air was so fresh every breath was like a cool glass of water.

13

In the summer of 2026 Scepticism Inc. took to the airwaves with its very own TV channel called Who Knows TV.

Edgar was filmed live from Sceptic Tower, limping about and encouraging viewers to phone in with their metaphysical convictions. He begged them, he implored them, he beseeched them to show him just how nutty they were.

They obliged him in droves. It was terribly sad really.

The three hundred telephone lines set up next to the studio

rang day and night. Bets appeared across the bottom of the screen as they were made, next to the message that Scepticism Inc. took all major credit cards.

On the very first night of Who Knows TV the Archbishop of Canterbury phoned so often he had to be asked to stop in order to allow other nuts to have a go.

Edgar made over thirteen million pounds in the first hour of Who Knows TV. He put on a great performance, urging all the nuts 'out there' to show him just how much they believed the things they couldn't prove. He was so animated, so vexed, so angry with all the nonsense people kept phoning in about. 'You fools,' he would say straight at the camera. 'Why do you do it? Why do you insist on giving me money for nothing? You're all fucking mad. I can't believe you people.'

He was sweating like billy-o under the studio lights and he kept damping his forehead with a tissue and his cheap suit became very very wrinkled.

Sometimes when he had had too much he would sit down on a massive white sofa covered in question marks and drink gallons of water or cups of tea. When pretty girls in white swimsuits and furry pink question marks on their heads handed him pieces of paper with the sums on, Edgar would inform his audience how much money he had taken off them so far. Sometimes he would stare off into space for minutes on end and then put his head in his hands and mumble about how there were so many nutty religious folk in the world it was a wonder anything ever got done. 'What,' he used to say, 'has absolute reality ever done for you?'

Other times he would try to explain his Guessing hypothesis and his Linguistic Relativity hypothesis but would get too worked up to get all the way through the arguments. Sometimes he would throw sofa cushions at the camera and repeat over and over again his little catchphrase, namely: put your money where your metaphysics are.

It was wonderful TV.

Edgar's first programme lasted four hours altogether. After the show a giant question mark appeared and the never-ending line of bets went across the bottom of the screen.

After the first night of Who Knows TV Edgar went straight to his bedroom. He was so exhausted that he needed to lean on me most of the way.

The floor of Edgar's bedroom was covered with dry leaves. He liked the noise they made when he moved through them.

On the ceiling over his bed was an enlarged photograph of Sophia Alderson praying.

Just as I was leaving Edgar asked me if I thought it would ever stop.

'What?' I asked.

'Religion, belief in things not known.'

'Who knows?' I said.

And Edgar said, 'Aloha.'

14

On the 5th of June 2026, the Archbishop of Canterbury called a press conference in the garden of Lambeth Palace and, as his wife served tea and biscuits, he announced matter-of-factly that as of ten o'clock that morning the Church of England was officially bankrupt.

15

Who Knows TV became the most popular TV station of all time.

Edgar began interviewing famous theologians. Typically he'd ask his guest some important religious question such as what is the true nature of God or how can I be said to have been a dung beetle in a former life? Or why does God forbid the eating of certain foods? Or in what way do the planets affect our personalities? Or why do paradoxical sayings bring us closer to truth? And then yawn and pretend to fall asleep on the couch next to his guest as they tried to explain such matters. Other times he would keep interrupting saying 'Who knows?' to canned laughter. Edgar would then invite his guests to make live metaphysical bets, thank them for coming on the show, express his opinion that they were mildly insane and give them a peanut suspended in a block of perspex.

Edgar asked Sophia Alderson to appear on his show. She responded by letter, saying that she would rather have both her arms pulled from their sockets by raging white stallions in Trafalgar Square.

Edgar wrote back and said he understood.

After handing his guest a peanut suspended in a perspex block Edgar would tell his millions of viewers to put their money where their metaphysics were.

And more meaningless claims were scrolled across the bottom of the screen.

Edgar would then read funny bits out of the Bible to yet more canned laughter. Some of the things Edgar read out of the Bible included:

But I tell you as a truth, there be some of them that stand here, which shall not taste of death, till they have seen the Kingdom of God. Luke 9:27

Behold, I will corrupt your seed, and spread dung upon your faces. Malachi 2:3

He that is wounded in the testicles, or have his penis cut off, shall not enter into the congregation of the Lord. Deuteronomy 23:1

Edgar's favourite passage of all from the Bible, was John 20:24 and was simply this:

Blessed are those who have not seen and yet have believed.

That little passage made Edgar laugh so hard his false eye would pop out, streams of tears would fall from his remaining eye and great globules of snot would slowly but surely sag from his nostrils. His chest would ache, his hands would shake, sometimes he even pissed himself after reading that little line out. It was great TV.

If Edgar was ever depressed, if say he was pining particularly badly for Sophia, I would just say 'John 20:24' and Edgar would be rolling around on the floor.

After he had read a bit from the Bible, Edgar would ask people to dig into their pockets for the sake of faith. 'I dare you,' he would say over and over again. And the phones kept on ringing with all manner of nuts on the other end desperate to part with their money.

Occasionally, Edgar would leap into a special part of the studio called Contradiction Corner, where he would read out two seemingly contradictory passages from the Bible. Such as:

I am one that bear witness of myself. John 8:18
and *If I bear witness of myself, my witness is not true.* John 5:31

161

or

> *I and my Father are one.* John 10:30
> and *I go unto Father; for my Father is greater than I.*
> John 14:28

Again to canned laughter.

After pleading with his audience to part with yet more money Edgar would stand in front of a blackboard and try to explain his Guessing hypothesis and his Linguistic Relativity hypothesis. It was during this part of the show that the most metaphysical bets were phoned in.

After that Edgar would pick up a holy text such as the Koran or the Vedic Scriptures and drop it on purpose repeatedly four or five times in a row, to canned laughter and drum rolls.

Edgar's show would end with him performing the Errr or with a close-up of the quote he had had tattooed on his left buttock.

Like I say, Who Knows TV became the most popular TV station of all time.

?

A week later a radio station similar in format to Who Knows TV was up and running offering to take religious people's money with the minimum of bother.

Who Knows TV and Who Knows FM eventually accounted for nearly half of all Scepticism Inc.'s absurd profits.

16

The archbishop's wife asked if any of the reporters would care for some walnut cake and the archbishop himself went on to say that the Church of England had spent something like fourteen billion pounds on various metaphysical bets supporting its doctrines and teachings. This was a truly stupendous amount of money, many times more than the Church actually possessed. The Church was deep in debt and had been for some time. Its creditors had demanded payment. Things, the archbishop said, had come to a head. The Church could no longer pay its ten thousand or so priests or maintain its property.

The archbishop said that he was going to see the Prime Minister. In the meantime every single church and cathedral owned by the C of E was to be closed until further notice.

The archbishop, when questioned, said that he had been aware of the financial crisis for some time but had decided to continue to place expensive metaphysical bets. He said he had done so with a clear conscience. 'I believed therefore I bet,' he said over and over again, then he made something of an impromptu speech. It went like this: 'We are all, of course, accountable to God. I absolutely fervently believe it was money well spent. Today is a glorious day to be a member of the Church of England. No other religion to date has come as close as we have to betting ourselves out of existence. We are the first! Bravo, I say. Our uncompromising zeal and total faith in Jesus Christ our Lord has outdone all the other religions in the world; we have truly put our money where are metaphysics are. Of this we ought to be duly proud. In light of scripture, the Church's actions has been most noble. I congratulate each and every priest and member of our flock who contributed in some way, no matter how slight, to our financial difficulties today. God bless you all.'

When he was asked what his feelings were now towards Scepticism Inc. the archbishop said this:

'I simply adore it. It's the most wonderful idea I've ever come across. We should have had it years ago. Let me tell you all something, I make no bones about it, when I go into one of those shops knowing that I am going to bet vast sums of money on minor details of dogma I feel wonderful. It's as if God is with me egging me on. I have felt closer to God in Metaphysical Betting Shops than anywhere else. They are the holy of holies. When I come back from placing a bet I'm ecstatic, my wife will tell you, I'd come home sometimes and I'd be so happy I'd find it impossible to sleep. It takes years off me.

'There's nothing to compare to making metaphysical bets, nothing on Earth, it's the best experience there is. Absolutely. You haven't truly lived until you have bet about a matter of faith.

'You know I once bet non-stop for forty-eight hours and it was just wonderful. I was as high as a kite. Betting is the most sacrificial way of showing one's obedience to God. It is nothing less than a form of Communion. I've even heard the Lord say, "Come now, Archbishop, surely I'm worth more than that," as I'm making a bet and of course he is. He is worth everything we have, and today we have gladly paid that price for him. Hallelujah!'

With that the Archbishop of Canterbury left Lambeth Palace, crossed Westminster Bridge and walked up Whitehall to Downing Street surrounded by a sea of frantic journalists. The medal Edgar had presented the archbishop flapped against his chest as he walked and got tangled up with his crucifix.

As news spread of the archbishop's announcement four Church of England clergymen hanged themselves in their belfries.

Aloha.

17

Negotiations at the Tashilhunpo Monastery dragged on and on.

In desperation, on the 24th of June the three Lamas headed back to Lhamo Latso, the Vision Lake.

Hundreds of journalists, the articulated lorry with the submarine and the mobile betting shop followed them.

?

On the 25th of June the leaders of every country in the world, the UN Secretary General, and major Scepticism Inc. shareholders gathered at Sceptic Tower to hear Edgar make a special announcement.

As the guests arrived Edgar and I greeted them at the main entrance, in the Hawaiian manner. I was introduced as a close friend. It was my first public appearance since the Great Mania, and the first time since the disaster that a conscious electrical appliance had been seen in public. Edgar reassured his guests that I was as sane as he was. The guests smiled nervously.

When everyone had arrived we mingled, as girls in white swimsuits with pink furry question marks on their heads walked around with trays full of glasses of champagne and little bowls of salted peanuts.

It was while I was talking to the Indian Prime Minister about hydro-electric power that Edgar sneaked up behind me and stuck a photocopy of my one and only metaphysical bet on my push-bar.

Everyone laughed. Edgar got on his knees and apologised profusely, saying that something had come over him.

?

Pope Ingram began a tour of Europe in Pope John John's Popemobile, which had been built from an old Soviet intercontinental nuclear missile carrier, weighed 340 tons, had a thirty-foot cross and was capable of sprinkling holy water in every direction.

Passing through the cities of Florence and Milan added ten million pounds to his bet. This brought his grand total to fifty-two million, the largest figure for any of the contesting Popes at the time.

18

The Panchen Lama and the sixteenth Dalai Lama climbed aboard the submarine on the Shugtri Ridge amid camera flashes, blessings and all sorts of metaphysical assertions. 'We'll be back in three shakes of a yak's tail,' promised the Panchen Lama as he was handed the sleeping seventeenth Dalai Lama by monks standing on the tops of ladders propped up against the submarine.

'We work it out,' said the sixteenth Dalai Lama as the ladders were taken away, the hatch closed and the crane on the articulated lorry swung the submarine over the Vision Lake. The sixteenth Dalai Lama was seen waving and grinning at a porthole. Then the submarine was lowered into the lake where it submerged and disappeared from view. All that was left of the three Lamas were bubbles on the surface of the Vision Lake.

Many said it was the single most important underwater voyage in the history of Tibetan Buddhism.

Eventually everyone took their seats and waited.

Time passed.

?

Edgar was called away to his office to talk with the Prime Minister. The Prime Minister wondered if Edgar would consider returning some of the money the Church of England had foolishly handed over to him. Edgar laughed. He laughed like this:

Ahhh-ooo Ahhh-ooo.

Then he said that unfortunately common decency prevented him from doing such a thing. It was impossible. The Prime Minister said he understood and the two of them left Edgar's office.

Back in the main lobby Edgar told jokes and showed his guests a number of metaphysical bets he particularly liked. One of these bets was the bet taken in the Jerusalem betting shop a week before for £500 that Yhwh is too sacred to pronounce aloud. Edgar read out that bet at least a hundred times. He loved it.

At twelve o'clock the little bowls of peanuts were completely empty and people were banging on the tables demanding something to eat. Edgar got up and walked to a microphone in the very centre of the lobby.

He tapped the microphone a few times, coughed and said this:
'Aloha. Metaphysical speculations are a waste of time. Mankind simply can't afford them. Metaphysics is the great inane human activity. I've spent my life trying to show this to be the case. Hardly anyone has paid any attention at all. There you go. What did I expect? I will keep trying, Ladies and Gentlemen, although I get very depressed about the whole thing.

'I honestly believe that the only time when metaphysical speculation could ever be morally justified is when we are no longer faced with pressing problems. Don't do metaphysics, I say, until life has become a great big bowl of cherries. Only when everything is just dandy should we even begin to think of wasting our time with metaphysical things. Metaphysics are for utopias only and even then we'd probably be better off without them. This much seems clear; we can't afford to play metaphysics yet, there are too many more pressing matters.

'Not long ago fifty million human beings were killed when conscious electrical appliances, such as my friend here, went berserk. I blame metaphysicians for that whole catastrophe, as I blame, in a less direct way, metaphysicians for many of the other self-inflicted catastrophes that mankind has endured over the ages. Fifty million human beings. Imagine that. You can't, it's too big a figure. It's not possible to grasp.

'Well, here is something else that's hard to believe, the same number of people who were killed in the Great Mania died in the last two years from hunger.

'I say this: talking about God, an afterlife, bickering over the nature of the Absolute, spending years and years considering the final resting-place of souls, spending one's life thinking how one is to achieve enlightenment and so on, indulging in the pointless pursuit of metaphysics, while fifty million people die for lack of food every two years is obscene.

'I have invited you all here tonight to announce that I, as of ten o'clock this morning, following intensive negotiations with some thirty-two countries, am the sole owner of all the major deserts of the world.

'That's right. All forty million square kilometres. Nearly a quarter of the total land mass of this nutty planet. Scepticism Inc. now owns the Sahara, the Arabian Desert, the Iranian Desert, the Touranian Desert in Ashia, the Thar Desert in India, the Takla Makan Desert in Mongolia and the Gobi Desert in China, the North American Desert covering parts of the south-west of the US and north-west Mexico, the Atacama Desert dividing the Andes from the Pacific Ocean, the Patagonian Desert in Argentina, and the Namib and Kalahari Deserts in south-western Africa, not forgetting of course the great Australian outback.

'I own the lot. Forty million square kilometres. That's more then can be properly imagined.

'I'm told I now own, among other things, the town of Calama. It's situated in the Atacama Desert, in what was, before ten o'clock this morning, part of Chile. I've never been to Calama. Maybe I never will. There's only one thing I know about Calama and I think it's quite a remarkable thing which I will now share with you all. It hasn't rained in Calama for over five hundred years.

'Soon we here at Scepticism Inc. will begin work on the first stage of our plan to turn these forty million square kilometres of sand into high-yield farmland. Our calculations show that this will roughly triple food production on this planet from 4,020 million metric tons to 12,000 million metric tons, enough to end hunger altogether.

'Our goal as always is this: the least pain and the longest life possible for as many as possible.

'We at Scepticism Inc. could, of course, with the ridiculous funds at our disposal, do just about anything we please. We could build a cathedral on the moon if we were nutty enough, and I hear that the Holy Church of Christ in Alabama is already saving for such a monstrosity. We could if we wanted to buy up several times over the South of France as George Milles Jr did. That was silly and pointless. George Milles Jr invented the Infinity Chip; for me that makes him the most gifted man ever and the closest thing to God there probably is, but he was still an arsehole. He squandered his wealth on himself and his countless identically named wives; he did nothing to help his fellow beings.

'Some will call our attempt to turn the deserts into farmland nothing more than a sensational act of self-publicity. This is perfectly true. I would want nothing more than for future history books to read something like this:

In the early twenty-first century a company founded by a man named Edgar Malroy took metaphysical bets and with the stupendous proceeds turned all the deserts in the world into farmland and wiped starvation from the face of the earth.

'That would be just fine by me.

'Others will say it is the work of a philanthropist. I like to think of it more as a conscious redirection of assets. A victory of common sense over madness. Of the physical over the metaphysical. Of the pressing over the irrelevant.

'What, I hear some of you say, of over-population? Well every year twenty stars like our sun are born within the Milky Way galaxy alone. We really ought to get out more.

'What begins now, the turning of desert into farmland, will not lead to a new Jerusalem; I am not about to create a new Eden, a heaven on Earth. What we envision doesn't come close to such corny, outlandish, nutty fantasies. Ours is a more modest goal. There will still be, no doubt, injustice, crime, death and sorrow when we have finished, but at least 500 million people will not perish for lack of food every two years. This is a modest goal when you think about it. It won't save people's souls for all eternity, it won't make us one with God, or let us reach Nirvana, or Enlightenment, or anything so grand, it just saves an incomprehensible number of people's lives. It is the least we can do.

'Thank you and Aloha.'

There was an outburst of clapping and cheering. Then the heads of state and shareholders promptly slipped out of the main lobby of Sceptic Tower to find any sort of restaurant that was open that late at night.

In no time the only people left in the main lobby besides Edgar, myself and Scepticism Inc. employees, who were picking up empty glasses and peanut shells, were a few nuts who wanted terribly for Edgar to take their money off them.

Edgar took their money looking more depressed about it than ever and then went straight to bed.

19

The next day the British government rushed an emergency Bill though the House of Commons. Known as the Restoration Bill, it promised the Church of England six billion pounds to help prevent its collapse. Many Members of Parliament objected to the Bill and it was passed with only the slimmest of majorities.

There was public outcry when it was realised that taxpayers would have to carry the can for the Church of England's zeal at the betting shop. Various Ban the Bill demonstrations were organised by angry taxpayers and the followers of other religions who objected to what they saw as favouritism and government bias. A number of such demonstrations ended in violent confrontations with the police and the Archbishop of Canterbury was pelted with rotten fruit wherever he went.

The government remained resolutely behind its Restoration Bill. The Prime Minister was something of a nut himself, as was most of his Cabinet.

The Church of England, even with the money promised in the Restoration Bill on its way, was hardly able to keep afloat. The archbishop, refusing to resign himself, was forced to sack scores of priests and sell off half of all the Church's property. This totalled some fifteen thousand parish churches and the cathedrals of Winchester, Sheffield, Brecon, Derby, Ely, Bristol, and Norwich.

As soon as they were put on the market, Edgar Malroy, to no one's great surprise, bought up every one of the churches and turned them into betting shops. The Archbishop of Canterbury was said to be delighted by this.

The cathedrals Edgar turned into storage depots for the countless receipts his company was acquiring at the rate of something like one hundred a second. Fourteen oil platforms in the North Sea had already been filled to the brim.

The archbishop also struck a number of lucrative sponsorship deals. Every single stained-glass window owned by the Church was removed and replaced with windows that had painted on them the words:

GLAXTON DOUBLE GLAZING
A family company with over 50 years' experience

Priests' gowns had the names of various companies sewn on them, like the jumpsuits of racing drivers. Most of the names that were sewn on priests' gowns belonged to insurance companies.

Edgar paid a seven-figure sum to have every priest of the Church of England, including the Archbishop of Canterbury himself, wear pink furry question marks on their heads.

Whenever any clergyman from the Church of England bowed his head in prayer, the furry pink question mark on his head would sway to and fro.

A moratorium on new priests was declared. But even after such drastic measures the Church found itself completely unable to continue payment of its pension scheme and some seven thousand retired priests and their families, along with five thousand widows, found themselves with no money at all.

It soon became a common sight all over the country to see old folk surrounded by grubby shopping bags sitting in town centres with bits of cardboard with the following sort of message written on them:

Retired C of E Priest.
Homeless hungry.

Those priests who had not been sacked were forced to take an eighty per cent cut in salary.

All kinds of money-making schemes were tried. The General Synod recommended that priests should wash their parishioners' windows for a competitive rate and soon it was a rare sight indeed to see a priest without a ladder over his shoulder and a bucket of soapy water in his hand.

172

Church of England priests cut their congregation's hair. They shaved them, treated their corns, give them back massages and facials, did their nails for them, and took home their washing and ironing.

Thousands of priests became part-time interior decorators, plasterers, plumbers and electricians.

'These are desperate times,' remarked the Secretary General of the Synod. 'Get out there and hustle.'

One priest in Liverpool had four massive coin-operated washing machines set up in his All Saints Chapel.

Some churches had pool tables, fruit machines and TVs installed. Others offered body-building gyms and tanning machines.

About four hundred priests applied for alcohol licences and nearly half of the churches still owned by the Church of England began offering a wide selection of freshly made sandwiches and other light snacks.

Some churches were turned into bedroom and kitchen furniture showrooms. The idea was that married couples would be able to buy what they needed as they got married.

Other churches were used as boarding kennels. Others became bowling alleys with automatic scoreboards and free coaching.

In Chichester a church cornered the local frozen ostrich leg market, with rows and rows of freezers in between the pews.

Priests became car dealers, or sold camping equipment, or crammed their churches with the highest quality carpets, rugs, cushion floors and vinyls, all at affordable prices.

Just about every single one of the money-making schemes tried by the Church of England turned out to be a dismal failure and lost yet more money. Priests seemed to be just terrible at doing anything practical.

Various committees reported to the General Synod failure after failure. Things looked bleak indeed. Another four priests were found hanging in their belfries.

Aloha.

A Lambeth Conference, held in Canterbury, was told of the Church's downward spiral. Everyone present prayed like billy-o. Only one church in the whole of England was found to be making a profit. That was the church in Chichester which was selling frozen ostrich legs at unbelievable prices.

It was then realised that there was one gap in the market which the Church of England ought to begin exploiting to the full. Every other scheme was abandoned and the whole Church put its weight behind the idea.

Within a month of the Lambeth Conference, the Church of England became the closest thing there was at the time to a chain of supermarkets.

20

The three Lamas remained submerged in the Vision Lake. Buddhists everywhere held their breath.

The sixteenth Dalai Lama and the Panchen Lama took it in turns to change the seventeenth Dalai Lama's nappies.

?

Sophia Alderson was outraged about the course the Church of England had taken.

She was beautiful when she was angry.

She told her followers God had never seen anything like it before. He was shocked. He was speechless. He was gutted. The Church of England had engaged in blatant commercialisation on a scale that not even Pope John John would have dared try.

God couldn't believe it, Sophia said. He was seriously considering another flood.

Sophia's followers kept on nodding.

Sophia, and the Blessed Virgin, placed the blame squarely on the Archbishop of Canterbury's shoulders for supping with the Devil, Edgar Malroy.

Sophia and her followers started picketing the churches-cum-supermarkets run by the Church of England as well as the Metaphysical Betting Shops. They booed anyone who came out of churches with shopping bags and tried to pull off the furry pink question marks the priests wore when they came to work on their bicycles.

Around this time Sophia published *Cosmic News Flash* part two. On the cover of *Cosmic News Flash* part two was a picture of Edgar Malroy with little red horns sprouting from his head.

The book, like its predecessor, was filled with bright pictures of shrines and the Virgin Mother. The book claimed that the prophecies written in the Book of Revelations were being fulfilled one after the other. Drastic steps had to be taken by the world's governments to avoid calamity, the book claimed. For one thing all wild animals had to be dressed in woollen trousers and waistcoats urgently. Nose-picking had to stop, as did a multitude of other things.

In the last chapter of *Cosmic News Flash* part two Sophia claimed that the Holy Mother of God had told her that Edgar's unholy mission, his goal, was nothing less than the destruction of religion. Sophia said the world had to act. All metaphysical bets should be made illegal. Edgar, she said, for the sake of mankind's eternal fate, had to be stopped.

Four million copies of the *Cosmic News Flash* part two were sold worldwide.

The profits went on wool, lots and lots of wool.

?

On the 15th of July 2026 the first religion in the world ceased to exist as a result of having overspent at the Metaphysical Betting Shop. Called Kamura, the religion was very small and hardly anyone had heard of it. Its founder, Andrew Temple from Birmingham, had phoned Who Knows TV and bet £400,000 that Kamura was completely true. In fact that was just about all anyone was ever able to find out about Kamura before it ceased to exist.

Edgar Malroy gave each and every one of his staff a bonus when he heard of the demise of Kamura. He and I then danced around his office.

By the end of the week another five esoteric and unheard-of religions were no more, having made one too many metaphysical bets.

Scepticism Inc. opened more Metaphysical Betting Shops in the premises that had formerly belonged to the religions that had bet themselves out of existence. Edgar bought a little black book which he kept in his cheap suit and wrote down in it the name of each of the religions that went to the wall.

Edgar would whip out the little book and read the names every two hours or so, making sure they had not disappeared, that he had not dreamed the whole thing. For the first time in a long while Edgar looked really happy.

Scepticism Inc. continued to move surplus food stocks to the places where the stuff was needed most in their fleet of ageing white ships with question marks on their bows and sterns. When New Guinea was hit by a massive tidal wave Scepticism Inc. led the relief effort. It funded literacy programmes in Guinea-Bissau, Mali, Ethiopia, Oman and the Upper Volta. It paid off Third World countries' bank loans, cared for refugees and prevented another four major wars, two attempted coups and untold civil wars by giving everyone involved in the disputes more money than they knew what to do with. Scepticism Inc. set up fifteen institutes to aid in the transfer of technology from the developed world to the developing world, increased its handouts to hospitals and continued to make the largest contribution to such organisations as the United Nations Children's Fund.

Scepticism Inc. also began building five massive digging machines which would, when finished, each weigh over twenty-thousand tons and would be the largest mobile land machines ever made.

?

Another General Council of the Roman Church was summoned and sat for three weeks. Rumour that a deal had been struck between the anti-chewing Popes was rife. Then on the 23rd of July the General Council made its decision known – it denounced the three current Popes for bickering and humiliating the Church, dismissed them for heresy and elected from their own midst a fourth Pope. A Cardinal Wilson.

All hell broke loose. Immediately Pope Ingram, Pope Morris and Pope Philips declared the General Council null and void. They said Pope Wilson's election was illegal.

The newly elected Pope Wilson demanded that all the other Popes acknowledge him as the true Pope. When they failed to do this he excommunicated the lot of them and placed a ridiculous amount of money on the bet that he was the Vicar of Christ, as was the custom for newly elected Popes.

This led to a frantic bout of metaphysical betting as Catholics all over the world backed their Pope with cash. In just twelve hours another twenty-two million pounds was spent on the question of which of the Popes really was God's messenger.

21

Sophia Alderson did not know what to say. She had Dr Cunningham push her in her wheelbarrow from one end of her room to the other for eight hours as she considered the implications of the new Pope. She just couldn't believe it. The Holy Mother was so upset, Sophia said, that her mascara had run.

Eventually Sophia fell asleep and Dr Cunningham, as he always did, tipped her lovingly into her bed.

?

Two hours after Pope Wilson had been elected a series of bubbles rose from the middle of the Vision Lake. The hordes of press and Tibetan Buddhists that ringed the lake took a step closer and squinted at the bubbles. The girls in the mobile Metaphysical Betting Shop got ready to take a stream of bets.

?

After Dr Cunningham had tipped Sophia into bed her room was filled with nuts and Dr Cunningham was hardly able to see Sophia's perfect, lovely bosom rise and fall. As the nuts made themselves comfortable in Sophia's room on the second floor of Rainthrope House, in the hope that she would mutter something interesting in her sleep, something remarkable happened.

Sophia Alderson for the very first time muttered something interesting in her sleep.

22

With a 'plup' noise the sixteenth Dalai Lama appeared gasping for air in the middle of the Vision Lake.

?

At first everyone in the room thought Sophia was saying the date for the end of the world. She was in fact mumbling in her sleep something else. She was mumbling this:

Oh, Edgar

?

With another 'plup' and then a slightly smaller 'plup' the Panchen Lama and the seventeenth Dalai Lama surfaced near to the spluttering sixteenth Dalai Lama.

The Panchen Lama and the sixteenth Dalai Lama shouted in Tibetan and then splashed water at each other.

The seventeenth Dalai Lama, resting in a life jacket, started to cry.

The Panchen Lama, still shouting at the sixteenth Dalai Lama, swam to the north shore of the lake with the seventeenth Dalai Lama where they were dried by their followers with big blue towels.

The Panchen Lama told reporters that the seventeenth Dalai Lama was the sole spiritual leader of Tibetan Buddhism and then promptly left for the Tashilhunpo Monastery.

After treading water for about half an hour the sixteenth Dalai Lama swam to the shore, punched a reporter on the nose and ran off down the mountainside dripping wet and laughing like mad, a small group of loyal monks following him.

During all the commotion that followed the mobile Metaphysical Betting Shop made a totally ridiculous profit. In fact it made so much money the former ice-cream van could hardly make its way down from the Shugtri Ridge.

?

Dr Cunningham snapped his clipboard in two.

?

On the 3rd of August 2026 another four minor religions were declared bankrupt as a result of overzealous metaphysical betting. They were the Church of Divine Light, based mainly in Brisbane, Australia; Boonkism, a branch of the Modimo religion of the Sotho-Tswana peoples of Southern Africa; the Chinese Church in London, and the Order of the Red Temple based in Bridgewater, which believed its members were reincarnated medieval tightrope walkers and controlled the destiny of mankind. These religions disappeared without trace. Edgar wrote their names down in his black book, performed a little jig, turned their places of worship into betting shops and then he and I flew to the US, in a white Scepticism Inc. jet, to inspect progress on the building of Edgar's five massive digging machines.

Things were coming along nicely.

?

A week later Pope Ingram arrived in Britain as part of his tour of Europe and headed straight to Sceptic Tower.

Edgar and myself greeted him on the steps outside. The Pope

offered Edgar his hand to kiss and Edgar said that he was trying to give up. Edgar then called the Pope a drag queen and gave him a bear hug. I said Aloha. Pope Ingram was chewing like crazy and thrust into Edgar's hand a cheque for twenty million pounds.

Then the Pope's massive entourage of three hundred priests, four hundred nuns, three hundred members of various religious orders, three hundred and fifty members of the Central Security Office and two hundred poleaxe-armed Swiss Guards appeared from Threadneedle Street.

They were all terribly exhausted. Some collapsed on the street; others sat on the steps in front of the tower or leaned against the Popemobile trying to catch their breath. They wore yellow mackintoshes and were all chewing like crazy.

Edgar and the Pope smiled at the cameras. Edgar said that of all the Popes, Pope Ingram was perhaps the nuttiest Pope of the lot and that was really saying something.

'You're too kind,' said Pope Ingram.

Edgar was about to say something else but stopped.

A frantic buzzing filled the street outside Sceptic Tower as across London Bridge marched thousands and thousands of Sophia Alderson followers shouting and nodding like crazy.

The mass of nuts were waving their illegible placards as if the world depended on it.

'Here she comes again,' said Edgar, blowing kisses to the love of his tragic life and leading the Pope inside Sceptic Tower.

I made sure I wasn't left outside this time.

The mass of nodding, drooling nuts halted in front of the Pope's entourage. There was a stand-off as the Pope's followers crossed themselves.

Sophia, sitting, as always, in her wheelbarrow, told reporters that

Pope Ingram was an imposter, a phoney, and a con man: the Mother of Jesus Christ had told her this at breakfast.

The thousands and thousands of Sophia's followers nodded like billy-o and waved their placards.

The three hundred priests, four hundred nuns, three hundred members of various religious orders, three hundred and fifty members of the Central Security Office and two hundred poleaxe-armed Swiss Guards crossed themselves again.

The Pope, shouting from the main entrance, told Sophia to go to hell. Edgar went on blowing kisses. Sophia ignored Edgar and commanded Dr Cunningham to push a way through the burly Swiss Guards in front of her.

Fighting broke out between Sophia's followers and the Catholic priests, nuns, Swiss Guards and security men soon after that.

Edgar phoned the police as things turned into a riot.

?

While the fighting was raging outside, Pope Ingram and Edgar appeared on Who Knows TV. The two men sat on the sofa covered in question marks drinking tea. Time passed. Screams and the smashing of windows could be heard coming from off the set. Edgar asked Pope Ingram (who as well as drinking tea was chewing a stick of Popegum and holding up the packet to the camera) to explain why he felt he was God's real messenger, the true successor to St Peter. As the Pope tried to explain his case, Edgar kept interrupting and saying, 'Who knows? Who really knows?'

'Who knows? I mean who really knows?'
   'I do,' said the Pope.
   'You know?'
   'Yes. I know.'
   'You think you know.'

'I know.'
'You think you know but you could be wrong couldn't you, your pompousness?'
'No. I know.'
'You think you know.'
'No, I know I know.'
'You know you know?'
'Yes.'
'You think you know you know.'
'No. I know.'
'How do you know you know you know?'
'I know.'

Outside the fighting raged. Neither side gave any quarter. Sophia's followers had the advantage of numbers, but the Pope's entourage were better armed. Things hung in the balance, neither side coming out on top. Time passed. There was a tremendous crash as the Popemobile was overturned by hundreds of livid nuts. The Pope's security men began firing their guns into the air and Dr Cunningham rammed Sophia's wheelbarrow into the row upon row of devoutly chewing Catholic priests. The Swiss Guards' casualties mounted.

Forty-five police vans arrived on the scene, sirens blaring.

Due to all the commotion outside Edgar and the Pope had to speak a little louder.
'You say you're the real Pope.'
'It is true.'
'You think it is true.'
'I know it is true.'
'You believe it is true.'
'I know it is true.'
'You believe you know it is true.'
'I know I know it is true.'
'How?'
'I *know*.'

'Who knows?'
'I know.'
'Who knows you know?'
'I do.'
'Oh yeah?'
'Yeah.'
'You're a nut, your pompousness.'
'I *know*.'

The Police Commissioner read out the Riot Act and then sent four hundred riot police into the theological fray.

Edgar poured the Pope another cup of tea, refused for the fifth time a piece of Popegum, showed the audience the cheque Pope Ingram had written out to Scepticism Inc. and presented the Pope with his receipt and a peanut in a perspex block.

?

In the end over three hundred arrests were made. Forty-five people were taken to hospital with various injuries including poleaxe and bullet wounds. High-ranking priests from the Vatican claimed diplomatic immunity.

Many of Pope Ingram's supporters who were arrested used their one phone call to make metaphysical bets on Who Knows TV in support of their Pope.

Sophia Alderson herself was detained for a while in New Scotland Yard but was released after every single policeman interrogating her fell hopelessly in love with her. Three became full-blown priests. The same thing had happened each time Sophia Alderson had been arrested for the attempted murder of Edgar Malroy.

23

The Church of England, exploiting the gap in the market caused by the demise of the supermarket business, began paying off its massive debts. The General Synod stated that the worst of the financial crisis was over. They forecast that by the year 2050 they would be out of the red altogether. The Anglican Church had come back from the brink.

On the 5th of August the Prime Minister, accompanied by the Home Secretary, arrived at Lambeth Palace and presented the Head of the Church of England with the six billion pounds as promised in the Restoration Bill.

Two hours later the Archbishop of Canterbury walked into the very first betting shop and blew the entire six billion on a single metaphysical bet.

The bet was this: God is love.

24

Receivers were called in and the Church of England ceased effectively to exist.

When Edgar heard what had happened he had every one of his employees in Sceptic Tower do the can-can in the main lobby.

The fifteen thousand churches, cathedrals and all remaining Church property were sold to Edgar Malroy.

The evening news showed rows and rows of former Anglican priests queueing up outside unemployment offices across the country. 'There is nothing quite as lovely, in my mind, as an unemployed priest. An unemployed priest is hope,' said

Edgar as we watched the news in the editing room of Who Knows TV.

That night Edgar held a service for the passing away of the Church of England on Who Knows TV. He spoke of an end of an era. He said the Church of England had gone somewhere better. He could hardly keep a straight face. He said that finally a gibbering voice had been silenced and that we were all one step closer to peace and quiet.

The former Archbishop of Canterbury phoned Who Knows TV and thanked Edgar for making it all possible. Edgar told the former archbishop that he had never known quite such an extraordinary nut as him before. 'If only there were more like you,' Edgar said.

The archbishop said he regretted nothing. He said he would do it again if he had the chance.

Live on TV, Edgar added the Church of England to the list in his little black book, grinning from ear to ear.

?

Sophia fell out of her wheelbarrow when she heard that the Church of England was no more.

Later she said she had seen it coming, as had, of course, the Virgin Mary. Sophia went on and on claiming that there was now absolutely no denying it: Edgar was the anti-Christ. It was plain as day. It was plainer than that.

Sophia spent the rest of the day the Church of England officially died planning how to stop Edgar and that night whispered his name in the sweetest voice you ever heard.

?

Edgar jerked off in his question-mark-shaped bathtub that night thinking of Sophia, as he did every night. At the moment of climax he screamed out, 'Than barwolowbikbikbik!' Sophia Alderson's name in tongues.

25

On the 7th of August Ayatollah Khorasani declared that it was an offence to Allah to place money on one's metaphysical beliefs. After he made this ruling he removed his 'I've put my money where my metaphysics are' badge and spat on it.

Other Muslim clerics and the influential Muslim World League backed the Ayatollah's ruling and spat on their badges so many times they became quite parched and had to stop and have something to drink. All over the planet Muslims engaged in a great deal of spitting.

The tide had begun to turn on poor old Edgar.

The collapse of the Church of England was a turning point for Scepticism Inc. It made the various religious leaders of the world sit up and ask themselves, for the first time, exactly why they were giving a confessed agnostic vast sums of money.

It was, if we are honest, a good question.

Edgar appeared on Who Knows TV and said how silly it was for Muslim leaders to ban metaphysical betting. He pointed out that the Koran insisted that all good Muslims should establish 'credit with God'. Now what better way was there to achieve this than with metaphysical bets?

Despite the fact that their spiritual leaders had banned metaphyical betting, hundreds and hundreds of Muslims phoned Who Knows TV and bet just as they had done before. They spent stupid sums of money on various bets relating to Islamic beliefs.

The urge to bet was just too great for Muslim nuts to resist, especially when an image of Edgar Malroy limping about and encouraging them in the peculiar way that he did, appeared on their TV screens. They couldn't help themselves.

?

It was a few hours later that the first bomb scare took place at Sceptic Tower. Edgar, his staff and myself stood outside in the rain next to Sophia Alderson's followers who kept on pointing at their illegible placards and telling us that we were in league with the Devil and so on.

The bomb disposal team took five hours to search the massive tower. No bomb was found. When everyone filed back in we heard that two Unitarian Churches with a total of ten thousand followers, two hundred priests and one hundred and fifty-two places of worship worldwide had ended. This brought tears to Edgar's remaining eye.

To be honest we were all rather moved.

I said Aloha.

And Edgar did the splits.

26

St Paul's Cathedral was turned, like all the other cathedrals throughout England, into a metaphysical betting receipts storage site. Within the space of a few days the whole of the vast building from the crypt to the whispering gallery was full of cardboard boxes containing receipts.

?

Pope Ingram cut short his tour of Europe when news of the death of Anglicanism reached him. After a five-hour meeting with his cardinals he appeared on the balcony overlooking St Peter's Square and declared himself to be the winner of the metaphysical dispute over which of the Popes was the true Pope. Pope Ingram thanked his supporters for their bets and said the matter had been successfully resolved. He had won. There was no need to continue betting.

Soon afterward Pope Philips issued a communiqué stating that it was God's will that his followers cease immediately betting at Metaphysical Betting Shops. He said the whole thing had been a stupid waste of money.

Pope Wilson also told his flock to refrain from betting.

But even after these announcements, money continued to be placed on their behalf at Metaphysical Betting Shops. Edgar, purely to annoy the Popes, went on phoning them up to tell them the latest ridiculous figures. Pope Philips soon refused to take the calls from London and Pope Ingram told Edgar to fuck off and die.

Hundreds of millions of Catholics simply found it impossible to stop betting.

?

On the 12th of August 2026, the first of Edgar's massive digging machines was finished. It looked like a sort of tortoise on wheels and was painted white with two giant blue question marks on its sides. It had a crew of fifty and was the size of a city block. Edgar named it Moses.

Moses was shipped on specially built barges to the Moroccan port of Safi, where it began at its top speed of ten miles per hour to head into the Sahara.

No one had seen anything like it.

Eight hundred miles and eight days later Moses stopped somewhere in what had been, before Edgar bought it, part of Algeria.

There Moses began digging the first of a series of connected kilometre-wide trenches which would eventually become part of a canal system to be filled with water from the Mediterranean.

Thirty Scepticism Inc. helicopters from specially built bases outside the town of Ain Salah flew in Moses' supply of fuel every day.

?

Disapproval of metaphysical betting grew and grew. Islamic leaders continued spitting and speaking out against it and Edgar quickly became known as the Great Infidel.

He loved it.

In the Regent's Park Mosque, devout Muslims kept pricking their feet on the pins of the thousands of discarded 'I've put my money where my metaphysics are' badges that littered the floor.

In Mecca Edgar's staff were asked to leave. The same thing happened to the betting shop next to Mohammed's tomb in Medina.

?

Pope Ingram appeared again on the balcony overlooking St Peter's Square and said metaphysical betting really had to stop. He said he was being perfectly serious.

In Jerusalem the Metaphysical Betting Shop was attacked by masked gunmen. In Japan Shinto priests conducted sit-in demonstrations against Edgar and his ridiculous business. Edgar began receiving hundreds of death threats a day from all over the world.

He took the whole thing really rather well. He told me he had been expecting it for a long time. Security was stepped up. Edgar went everywhere in a white armoured car and hired numerous bodyguards.

?

By the 14th of August another seventeen religions no longer existed thanks to Scepticism Inc. So many religions were going to the wall, in fact, that the BBC had a special part of the six o'clock news devoted solely to the subject.

Every night on Who Knows TV Edgar would say a few words about the religions that had that day ceased to exist; he would say that they had gone somewhere better. Then he would implore his audience to bet on their metaphysical convictions and they did in vast numbers.

Every time a religion was declared bankrupt on the news, Sophia Alderson would fall out of her wheelbarrow in shock. 'I can't believe this is happening,' she would say to the Virgin Mother. They agreed that Scepticism Inc. had to be stopped.

Every single religion on the planet quickly found itself in financial difficulty. Funds just dried up. The supermarket within the walls of the Vatican was shut, the leaders of the Eastern Orthodox Church were said to be living off lentil soup, and Ayatollah Khorasani's diet consisted mainly of figs.

Christians in China were eating peanuts again.

191

?

It was around this time that Edgar announced that he was turning a former Church of England theological college in Kent into Who Knows College, where he intended to train future employees of Scepticism Inc. in the business of metaphysical bet taking.

By the end of the year more than forty people had received agnosticism diplomas from the 180-acre facility. Including me.

?

Although just about every single religion had forbidden its followers from placing metaphysical bets, Edgar's profits increased. It wasn't just members of the congregations that went against their Churches' wishes, priests found themselves sneaking off to betting shops, often at the dead of night, desperate to spend sizeable amounts of cash on their religious beliefs. They couldn't stop themselves. Anything of value churches possessed started disappearing. Vatican security men were ordered to frisk each and every priest who left the Holy City. Hundreds were caught trying to smuggle out statues, gold plates, jewels, film equipment and just about anything else of value.

?

Shinto priests said that betting on metaphysical convictions was 'unnatural'.

Sikhs said it was an offence.

A spokesman for the Ethiopian Orthodox Church said betting on one's religious beliefs was obscene.

Hindu Brahmans said betting was unclean and had to stop and eight Chief Rabbis said enough was enough.

?

A series of emergency ecumenical meetings were held to discuss the deepening crisis. These meetings denounced metaphysical betting in the strongest terms possible. Those present at such meetings prayed like billy-o that betting would die out. They said governments had to do something.

?

Pope Philips published an encyclical denouncing all metaphysical bets as insults to the glory of God. Any Catholic who bet was to be excommunicated at once.

Even after Pope Philips had published his encyclical the amount of money Edgar received from nuts on the Pope's behalf continued to grow.

Things were out of control.

On the orders of Pope Ingram, Popedoms were doubled in price.

?

One night shots were fired at Sceptic Tower from a speeding car. No one was hurt.

Two nights after that, in what looked like a well-organised operation, thirty-three Metaphysical Betting Shops were set alight across the American bible belt. Several Christian militia organisations claimed responsibility.

Scepticism Inc. staff, in addition to their white swimsuits and furry pink question marks that bobbed to and fro on their heads, were issued with bulletproof jackets.

'The show must go on,' Edgar said.

27

On the 25th of August I left London to enrol at Who Knows College. Before I left I said goodbye to Edgar. As he would be giving the lectures, saying goodbye was a little pointless but I felt like it. He was sitting at his altar/desk twiddling with his Geiger counter that didn't have any batteries in. He looked very small even with his bulletproof jacket and white helmet on. He was mumbling to himself, 'The Rastafarian Church has come out against us, as has the Church of Scientology and it's only a matter of time before the International Assembly of Baptists denounces us. They all hate me. There was a time when they would have fallen over themselves to shake my hand or have their photograph taken with me but not now. It's all changed. Do you know what I say? I say it's about bloody time. Those fucking nuts have only just realised what's going on! They've only just realised there's a cat amongst the pigeons!'

Edgar got up and limped around his room shaking his head and every now and again waving his good arm in the air.

'They've only just seen what I'm up to. Can you believe it? They thought I was offering them a service. Well it's finally dawned on them: this is war! It's them or me. The world isn't big enough for the both of us; it's religion or it's Scepticism Inc. And you know what – we're actually winning.' Edgar waved his black book at me. 'Can you believe it? The receiverships speak for themselves; we're beating the metaphysician at his own game. It's unbelievable, stupendous! It's a great time to be alive! I had hoped that some time in the distant future something like this would happen, but so soon? I mean another six today and it's not even eleven.'

Edgar began reading out names from his book.

'The Holy Church of God, the Ukrainian Autocephalous Orthodox Church, the Divine Grace Church, and the Shilluk religion of south Sudan. The Church of – '

'Edgar, I have to go. The coach is going to leave.'
'I'll be along a bit later.'
'See you there then.'
'Aloha.'
'Aloha.'

?

On the 3rd of September the second of Edgar's massive digging machines was completed. It was named Jesus by Edgar and shipped overland to the Mojave Desert in what had previously been part of North Mexico. Once it was in the very centre of the wasteland it began digging like billy-o.

?

Fourteen Swiss Guards were ordered by Pope Ingram to escort Edgar's employees out of St Peter's Square. The empty betting shop was then set alight by cardinals with Zippos.

Within hours Edgar had opened new betting shops just outside the Vatican in what had been trattorias. The trattorias had been forced to sell up when their clientele, the priests of the Vatican, couldn't afford to eat out any more.

Pope Ingram spoke to the Italian Prime Minister about the matter. He said that the Vatican was virtually surrounded by betting shops and that this was a provocative act on the part of Scepticism Inc. The Pope said it amounted to a siege.

?

About a month after the final demise of the Church of England, supermarkets began reappearing around the world.
For the first few weeks hardly anyone went inside them.
Eventually, though, people started shopping again. Everyone kept breaking down as memories of the Great Mania came

flooding back and the new supermarkets quickly sold out of tissues.

I never ventured into the new supermarkets. I just couldn't do it.

28

While Sophia and the Virgin Mother schemed Ayatollah Khorasani had vans with loudspeakers drive through the bazaars of the Arab world broadcasting his disapproval of metaphysical betting. Muslim priests, after calling the faithful to prayer from minarets, would add:
    'And remember whatever you do, don't bet.'

On the 6th of September the Afro-West Indian United Council of Churches, with an estimated forty thousand members, concluded that it was 'remarkably foolish to make metaphysical bets'.

The Union of Welsh Independents, which a week before had lost half of its ministers due to debt caused by metaphysical betting, declared the whole thing 'a ruse of the most despicable order'.

The same day 1,025 former places of worship were put on the market when the Free Church folded due to impossible financial difficulties.

?

The inaugural lecture of Who Knows College went something like this:
    About thirty students and myself sat in the damp, brown lecture theatre. An absence of dust showed where, before, a giant cross had been hung on the wall.

?

Two hours earlier the Independent Methodists had ceased to exist, and the United Synagogue had made a statement claiming that metaphysical betting was the silliest thing it had ever heard off. That morning the *Financial Times* had printed an article claiming that the Vatican Bank, the Institute for the Works of Religion, was close to calling in the receivers. This the Vatican strongly denied but Pope Ingram, during a lunchtime appearance on Italian TV, asked all elderly Catholics who intended to leave money to the Church in their wills, to kindly hand over their gifts immediately.

?

Everyone had their pens and notebooks out. Edgar limped into the room still wearing his bulletproof jacket and helmet, waved at us and said Aloha.

We said Aloha back. Then Edgar stood behind his lectern and said:

'There is not enough love and kindness in the world to permit us to give any of it away to imaginary beings, such as God.'

It was, like so much of what Edgar said, a paraphrase of Friedrich Nietzsche.

After that Edgar talked about the similarity of religion to sport, the fact that they both generally took place at weekends, both used language no one else seemed to understand, involved men wearing stupid-looking costumes and most importantly revolved around utterly meaningless rules and conventions.

At one point during his inaugural lecture, when Edgar asked if there were any questions, a student at the back asked about miracles.

Edgar said that only a really hardcore nut could believe, or even want to believe, that a God would intervene in the world in utterly

197

stupid little ways, curing a head cold here, a brain tumour there. Edgar Malroy said that such a God would have to be hysterical and incontinent. Edgar said that those who believe God will remove verrucas from the faithful while letting the non-believers die of starvation in their millions needed serious medical attention.

Edgar said that such a God would have to be abolished if he existed and that places like Lourdes ought to be evacuated and then carpet bombed.

29

At ten o'clock at night on the 8th of September a blue van was parked outside Sceptic Tower. Twenty minutes later the van exploded, shattering every window for half a square mile.

At the precise moment the van exploded Edgar yelled, 'Than barwolowbikbikbik!' He was found unhurt by firemen in his bathtub on the 145th floor. It had been a near thing. Edgar, still in his bathtub shaped like a question mark, was carried out of the damaged tower by six firemen, two of whom Edgar noticed wore 'I've put my money where my metaphysics are' badges.

Repair work on Sceptic Tower was started the next day and by the end of the week it was as if the whole thing hadn't happened.

?

Religious leaders all over the world continued to voice their opposition to metaphysical betting.

The Dutch Reformed Church said Scepticism Inc.'s unacceptable and unchristian activities had to be stopped immediately by whatever means. Shi'ite Muslim clerics burned effigies of Edgar in the streets of Tehran and Bradford and the Seventh

198

Day Adventists called metaphysical betting 'the pastime of imbeciles'.

Edgar agreed wholeheartedly with the Seventh Day Adventists.

Despite the widespread opposition of religious leaders to Scepticism Inc., nuts all over the world kept on betting like crazy. They couldn't help themselves. They would sneak off to betting shops and hand over their money time and time again. The number of MBOs reported rose steadily and Metaphysical Betting Anonymous became the largest self-help organisation in the world.

?

On the 10th of September the Vatican switched off its electricity. Pope Ingram denied that this had anything to do with Scepticism Inc. 'We think candles are holier, that's all,' he told reporters in the dark.

On the 11th of September, amid very tight security, Edgar took myself and the other students from Who Knows College to see St Paul's Cathedral jam-packed with cardboard boxes containing metaphysical betting receipts.

'But Edgar,' I said after I had been carried up the 259 steps to the Whispering Gallery, 'there's nothing to see. The dome, the frescoes, everything's hidden behind the boxes.'

'Isn't it fantastic!' Edgar said, his voice full of emotion as he slapped the cardboard boxes that filled the second largest dome in the world.

With all the boxes, to be heard on the other side of the Whispering Gallery you had to shout.

?

On the same day that Edgar showed us around St Paul's, the Church of the New Jerusalem was declared bankrupt as a result of metaphysical betting.

Two days later the Christadelphians folded as well.

199

A week later and the Scientologists had outbet themselves.

They were followed by the Seventh Day Adventists, who had only recently declared metaphysical betting to be the pastime of imbeciles, the Yoruba religion of Nigeria, a branch of Voodoo in Haiti and the Disciples of Christ whose origins went back to the eighteenth century.

?

Zen Buddhists officially banned, and at the same time officially encouraged, metaphysical betting.

Sikh Granthas and Hindu holy men added their voices to the protest against Scepticism Inc. They said only fools would place metaphysical bets and they were probably right.

The Krishna Consciousness Movement stated in a press release that people should chant all the time rather than bet. Two days later the Krishna Consciousness Movement stopped chanting for good. Edgar wrote the name down in his little black book. Twice.

?

Sophia Alderson insisted that the world had to 'beg not bet'. If people went on betting, she warned, mankind would be terribly punished by the All Forgiving God. She believed this with all her nutty beautiful heart. Every day the Virgin Mother reminded her what was at stake if Edgar was not stopped. Sophia issued statement after statement, press release after press release, condemning metaphysical betting. On the chat shows she appeared on she refused to talk about anything else. She said that people had to stop betting immediately, that God didn't like being made a fool of.

200

Who knows?

Sophia's warnings, like the warnings of all the other religious leaders, seemed to fall on deaf ears, for all over the planet millions and millions of religious nuts kept on handing over, with wild abandon, totally unbelievable sums of money in support of their metaphysical views.

'It simply can't last,' Sophia said. God was at the end of his tether.

?

Edgar lectured to us on all manner of things. He told us about his Guessing Hypothesis, how no metaphysical assertion was any better than any other. That there exists an all-powerful being outside of space and time was no more likely than that there exists outside space and time a ponderous haddock. 'Anything could be out there. The universe may be shaped like a giant vagina for all we know. The priest, the metaphysician, stands in his pulpit and tells us what's going on when in fact he's just guessing or, even worse, repeating someone else's guess. These guesses aren't even educated guesses. They can't be. The metaphysician doesn't know what the hell he is talking about, religion is just a series of utterly blind guesses; that is to say, religion is bullshit.'

Edgar paused so that we could write down what he had said. Given my ZEm 12000 Nexus memory system I didn't need to.

'Do you have any idea how many nuts have declared themselves to be God's messenger? Have you? It's utterly breathtaking. Do you know how many denominations there are in Christianity alone? Over twenty-two thousand. Each one claiming it alone is mumbling on about the Truth. What a fucking joke.'

Edgar said there was a Messiah born every minute.

30

As Edgar was returning to Sceptic Tower after reopening a betting shop in East London which had been firebombed the night before, a limpet mine blew his armoured car into the air. Sixteen people were seriously hurt, around twenty bystanders were slightly injured, three buildings were reduced to rubble and something like twenty cars were set on fire.

Edgar walked away from the scene with minor head injuries.

He was kept in St Antony's Hospital overnight for observation.

?

The next day, in full view of thousands of followers filling St Peter's Square, Pope Ingram ripped up every single metaphysical betting receipt he had ever received. He also smashed the peanut in the perspex block that Edgar Malroy had presented him about a month before on Who Knows TV.

Everyone in St Peter's Square crossed themselves.

After Pope Ingram had ripped up his metaphysical receipts he fed them to thirty-two hamsters in thirty-two white cages that took up most of the balcony. Pope Ingram urged all God-fearing Catholics to do the same.

?

Following the sacking of eight thousand priests and members of the Roman Curia at the Vatican, an official announced that until further notice all beatifications and canonisations were to be suspended due to a shortage of manpower. A little later that same day Pope Ingram appealed to his followers to give charitably to the Church. 'We can't run on Hail Marys alone,' he said.

?

Radio Vaticana, which broadcast to some two hundred countries in thirty-five languages for sixteen hours a day, went off the air.

?

The Patriarch of Constantinople said he never wanted to see another pretty girl in a white swimsuit for as long as he lived.

?

Popedoms became very expensive.

?

The religious crisis deepened. Some fifteen per cent of all known religions had disappeared due to the activities of Scepticism Inc.

As much as the priests shouted at them, shook them, slapped them and preached against betting from their pulpits, nuts went on betting and betting. It was too late. They simply loved it. Perhaps, if the religious leaders had tried to ban betting earlier they might have met with more success, but, as it was, betting on one's metaphysical convictions had become something of a habit, a planet-wide pastime, that proved impossible to stop. Until the very end.

As things got worse and worse vast numbers of livid, bedraggled, suddenly unemployed priests flocked to Sceptic Tower in protest at their fate. Most were speechless with rage, furious that Scepticism Inc. had reduced them to little more than beggars. Every day at lunchtime Scepticism Inc. staff would hand out bowls of soup and hunks of bread to the former priests, who were so livid they could hardly swallow.

As the death toll of religions grew, more and more holy men joined the bedraggled, fuming crowd that stood under the shadow of the giant question mark. The new arrivals looked like they had been shipwrecked in some terrible storm.

?

The next month another sixty-one religious denominations were wiped from the face of the Earth. Five native American religions died out all on the same day and the occult following of Ouspensky ran out of money as did the Muggletonians. The Popes were said to be incredibly hard up and the Panchen Lama was using reusable nappies.

31

Edgar lectured us on why religion was so funny.

'It isn't just because religion takes itself so seriously,' he said. 'Religion by its very nature is absurd, it can't help it. Religion is the greatest joke of them all. It's the funniest thing there is. It is the longest running joke in the history of the world. Mankind has been telling itself the joke for millennia.'

The trouble was, Edgar said, that man has been telling the joke for so long he's forgotten to laugh.

Edgar said part of the reason for Metaphysical Betting Shops was to make us laugh more at the crazy things religion said were so.

He told us to consider, for example, the Trinity. One but Three at the same time.

When Edgar Malroy first heard about the Trinity he nearly died laughing.

Reincarnation cracked him up as well, all of it did, the idea of a Soul, of God. But the funniest thing of all, the thing that really took the biscuit, was blind faith itself.

'I doubt wherever you end up you'll ever come across anything half as funny or as scary or as stupid or as sad as blind faith,' Edgar said, grinning.

He then wrote the following words on the blackboard:

'Blessed are those who have not seen and yet have believ – '

He didn't manage to finish the quote because he was laughing so much his false eye popped out of its socket, bounced off the blackboard and down the throat of a former Catholic in the third row.

An ambulance was called when the poor girl passed out.

?

The Lefters, a religious movement that had broken away from orthodox Winboism during Edgar's time at Tewkesbury University, stopped peddling its curious brand of nuttiness due to financial pressure brought about by metaphysical betting.

Edgar was visibly relieved. Since I had met him he had rarely talked about the religion he had inadvertently founded in his college days. He was embarrassed about the whole thing. He was utterly ecstatic when he was informed a week later, recovering in hospital, that orthodox Winboism was also no more.

Edgar was recovering in hospital at the time from another attempt on his life.

What had happened was this:

Someone had placed near the central ventilation system of Sceptic Tower four canisters of nerve gas.

Edgar, one hundred and fifty of his employees and three hundred nutty customers were taken to hospital.

Tyre marks were found near the scene of the crime which matched perfectly the single tyre of Sophia Alderson's wheelbarrow.

The police arrested Dr Cunningham as he left a men's outfitters.

32

Dr Cunningham confessed to everything.

Between Dr Cunningham's arrest and trial a further twenty-eight religions had died off. He told his lawyer that he had done what he had done because he was in his professional opinion out of his mind. He was, he said, hopelessly in love. Love was his alibi.

At his trial the public gallery was festooned with illegible placards.

When the jury found Dr Cunningham guilty the judge said that Dr Cunningham was a total disgrace to psychiatry and a danger to the public. He sentenced him to fifty years in prison.

When Sophia Alderson heard of the verdict she declared it contrary to the Law of God. She then promptly declared Dr Cunningham a saint.

Outside Rainthrope House reporters wanted to know if it was Dr St Cunningham or St Dr Cunningham.

Who knows?

33

During St Dr Cunningham or Dr St Cunningham's trial the six-teenth Dalai Lama parachuted on to the Tashilhunpo Monastery with four hundred followers. Every single one of them was armed with guns. Big old Chinese guns.

The Panchen Lama later claimed that most of the sixteenth Dalai Lama's followers were in fact mercenaries. The sixteenth Dalai Lama denied this, saying it was silly.

Mercenaries or not, the sixteenth Dalai Lama's men successfully stormed the monastery with only minor losses, but the sixteenth Dalai Lama's real quarry, the seventeenth Dalai Lama, managed to escape and was already on the Orient Express guarded by five of the Panchen Lama's most trusted monks bound for Switzerland.

When news of the seventeenth Dalai Lama's escape reached the sixteenth Dali Lama he laughed like crazy.

The monks of the Tashilhunpo Monastery, formerly loyal to the Panchen Lama and the seventeenth Dalai Lama, were marched to the betting shop at the base of the monastery where they were forced to place vast sums of money on the metaphysical bet that the sixteenth Dalai Lama was the real spiritual leader of Tibetan Buddhism.

Edgar subsequently declared such bets null and void because they had been made under duress.

The sixteenth Dalai Lama told reporters that the storming of the Tashilhunpo Monastery was nothing. In a former life he had been present at the siege of Stalingrad. 'Now that was something,' he said.

Within days a sizeable army of supporters of the Panchen Lama and the seventeenth Dalai Lama marched on Tashilhunpo. In overall command was the Panchen Lama himself. For three days and nights the monastery was shelled by a battery of mountain guns last used in 1879 by the Afghan army. After this bombardment monks loyal to the Panchen Lama assaulted the monastery with wicker chairs.

The sixteenth Dali Lama and his men drove off repeated attacks but things were not looking good; ammunition was running out and the number of Tibetan Buddhists betting on the old Dalai Lama's cause was at an all-time low.

?

As the fighting continued at the Tashilhunpo Monastery, the Methodist Church, with over forty million adult members, was proclaimed insolvent, as were fourteen Baptist Churches, most of them in the United States, while in Battersea Park Buddhists burned an effigy of Edgar Malroy next to the Peace Pagoda.

34

The ancient mountain guns were preparing to fire again on the Tashilhunpo Monastery when Edgar and I flew in in a white helicopter with question marks on its doors. I was crammed full of money which Edgar gave out to everyone in sight. At first the Panchen Lama refused to talk to Edgar, but eventually Edgar managed to get both sides to agree a ceasefire and a little later negotiated terms for a total cessation of fighting.

The terms for the total cessation of fighting were these: if the sixteenth Dalai Lama and his men put down their arms, they would be allowed to leave the country.

Edgar told the sixteenth Dalai Lama that it was the best that he could do.

Edgar, the sixteenth Dalai Lama and myself left the smoking remains of the Tashilhunpo Monastery in the helicopter an hour later. Edgar and the sixteenth Dalai Lama argued about karma and the five realms of the wheel of life non-stop for twelve hours as we flew back to London in a Scepticism jet. There the sixteenth Dalai Lama was interviewed on Who Knows TV and given a peanut in a block of perspex.

All during his interview on Who Knows TV the sixteenth Dalai Lama had been covered head to foot in bits of plaster from the Tashilhunpo Monastery.

?

Every single mosque in Tunisia was closed due to a lack of funds. A day later Ayatollah Khorasani in Iran issued a fatwa calling for the death of Edgar Malroy for his impudence to Allah. The fatwa went like this: 'Edgar Malroy is a very serious infidel. We have issued a decree against him. He must be killed. God is Great.'

When news of the fatwa reached Edgar he said that it was about time too.

35

A few hours after the Ayatollah had issued his fatwa, Pope Philips issued an encyclical that seemed to be saying in the politest language possible that Edgar ought to be burned at the stake.

?

The Patriarch of Constantinople called Edgar an 'arsehole'.

?

At roughly the same time the third massive digging machine was finished. Amid very tight security Edgar named it Mohammed. Specially built barges then transported Mohammed to what had formerly been part of Chile. There it began digging, as the other two machines were, a series of interconnected kilometre-wide trenches.

?

Edgar appeared on Who Knows TV and begged his viewers to keep sending in their money, to keep betting on their religious convictions.

Edgar gave his last remaining appearances on Who Knows TV everything he had. Perhaps he suspected that the whole thing was about to come to an end.

He was just wonderful to watch; jumping around, laughing, clenching his fists, sweating, swearing, dribbling, moaning, pleading. He broke down and cried live on a number of occasions. It was wonderful TV.

Millions and millions of pounds kept pouring into Scepticism Inc.

Edgar raved on and on every night, criticising the world religious leaders for banning metaphysical betting. He said he couldn't see why they would even consider doing such a thing, unless of course they didn't believe the nutty stuff they went on about as much as they made out.

'What are you to think of priests who don't put a single penny of their own money on the nonsense they peddle but expect you to make contributions every single Sunday?' Edgar asked his audience as he relaxed on the couch covered in question marks sipping from a cup of tea.

'You know what I would say if I were you?' said Edgar, peering at the camera. 'Next time you see your priest, I'd say this: "Put your goddam money where your metaphysics are!"'

Edgar threw his cup of tea at the camera. Then he jumped up and shook the camera, shouting for his audience to wake up.

?

Scepticism Inc. launched a worldwide advertising campaign to combat the bad press it was getting from those religious leaders still in business. The posters said:

> How do you know God doesn't want you to bet?

and

> Go on, for God's sake, bet.

Many of the thousands of posters were vandalised as soon as they were put up but the message got through; the number of bets rose.

?

On the 25th of October three employees of Scepticism Inc. were killed when a car bomb went off outside a Metaphysical Betting Shop in Swindon.

On the 27th, a Scepticism Inc. employee was seriously injured when a follower of Sophia Alderson stabbed her while pretending to place a bet.

The next day a follower of Sophia Alderson gunned down four 'lost ones' queuing outside a betting shop in Leeds in an attempt to save their souls.

Drive-by shooting of betting shops occurred in Los Angeles every five minutes.

Such events forced Edgar to increase security yet again. Electrified fences were erected around betting shops and patrolled by guard dogs.

On the 28th, a betting shop in New York was blown sky high when a suicide bomber drove a truck laden with explosives into the building. Twenty-five members of staff and over fifty nuts were killed. Eye witnesses reported that the suicide bomber was smiling when he drove into the building.

Forty-eight extremist religious groups, from every remaining major religion on the planet, claimed responsibility.

Edgar flew to New York to supervise the funerals and the rebuilding work. He then flew to the Sahara to inspect the work of the first digging machine, Moses.

Moses had excavated 270 million square metres of sand.
   Moses' handiwork was visible from space.

Things were coming along nicely.

36

Edgar lectured us about the need for a metaphysics-free morality. A morality based on something physical rather than metaphysical. A bullshit-free morality. 'Forget rewards and punishments, those sort of things are for the nuts. Being kind due to a fear of God is expediency not morality. And anyway what could possibly be worse than heaven?' he said. Edgar believed that a bullshit-free morality would come into being when we looked honestly at death.

?

All four Popes met in Helsinki. It was the first time since the beginning of the Second Great Schism that they were all together. They put their names to a document that damned Edgar Malroy and anyone who worked for him to hell for all eternity. It was the only thing the Popes could seem to agree on.

?

'I will be no more. So will you. We are mortal, we are in deep shit. And that's the point, we are in the shit together. We are all going to die. Everyone should wear watches that every now and again beep and have written on their liquid crystal displays: "You are about to die." Because we are. Such watches would, in a small way, help us remind ourselves that we are all finite, that we will die, and that consequently we ought to live for the moment.

'Only religious nuts want to die. Early Christians were queuing up to get in the amphitheatre, literally queuing up. They failed to see their own finitude. They believed they would exist for ever, they thought that things can be put off; well, they can't.

'Every time you meet someone think: "This person is not perfect, is not just how they want to be, this person will never complete all his or her projects. This person is not loved by friends and family as much as he or she would like. This person regrets. Misses. This person will sometime soon be dead. Perhaps in the next half hour. Perhaps in thirty years. Who knows?"'

Edgar Malroy told us to imagine everyone we ever met dead. He told us to imagine the blood falling away from their faces, to imagine that their feet would never walk again, to imagine their eyes closed permanently and their eyelashes perfectly still. He told us to imagine their clothes hanging neatly on wire hangers in coroners' offices.

'And if you don't feel, after you've thought these things, after you have accepted completely the other person's finitude, like hugging them, well, then you're dead already.'

The lecture theatre was completely still. The only sound we could hear was the muffled noise of the former priests outside Who Knows College shouting themselves blue in the face about how Edgar had tricked the faithful into handing over their money.

After his lecture on death Edgar threw peanuts to the former priests from a window of Who Knows College.

?

Sceptic Tower was bombed three more times before the end of October. Edgar lived through all the attacks sustaining only minor injuries.

The Catholic Church of Lithuanians in London went bust.

Shintoism stopped being practised altogether and the number of Pentecostal churches in the United States of America dropped by eighty-eight per cent.

On the 30th of September the Society of Friends stopped collective worship. The House Church Movement died out, one hundred Lutheran Churches all over the planet were put up for sale and the Spiritualist Church gave up the ghost.

Popedoms were being sold for £24.99 a go.

?

A fourth digging machine was completed, named Shiva and shipped to Walvis Bay on the tropic of Capricorn. From there it moved overland to the centre of the Kalahari Desert in what had formerly been part of Botswana.

A little later Scepticism Inc. completed a fifth digging machine which Edgar called Buddha.

Buddha was sent to what had been, before Edgar had bought it, part of Mongolia. There it began carving out a series of kilometre-wide trenches in the Gobi Desert. Trenches that were to be filled with water from the Sea of Japan. It never happened.

37

In the United States of America not a single TV evangelist remained in business.

?

On the 15th of November 2026 a meeting took place at Rainthrope House. All morning a series of cavalcades arrived. As each guest stepped into the grounds of Rainthrope House thousands of nuts nodded like crazy at them.

The list of religious leaders present at the meeting was impressive. Effectively, the heads of what was left of every religion on Earth gathered in a building on the outskirts of London that had been built to house the mentally ill.

They assembled in the dining room. Most sat on plastic orange chairs that were really too small for adults. Some sat cross-legged. Hindu holy men, who had renounced sitting down in order to attain Liberation, kept being asked to get out of the way. Yogis leaned upside-down against the wall for the entire length of the meeting.

Sophia Alderson chaired the proceedings. She did so because she was beautiful and because she felt she was God's messenger. She told the assembled religious leaders that things had gone on for long enough. She scolded them for being complacent, for actually placing so many bets themselves and for being such bad examples to their followers. She insisted that nothing like this would have

215

happened if everyone had listened to her. No one at the meeting felt like disagreeing with her.

Sophia Alderson then had one of her followers turn on a slide projector. Sophia showed her guests a series of bar charts and financial forecasts for each of the remaining major religions. She predicted that if metaphysical betting continued at its current rate, twenty of the twenty-five major religions would be bankrupt within a month. The rest would follow in a year at the very latest.

The dining room was filled with gasps and tuts.

Sophia quieted her audience then she said that such an outcome was clearly unacceptable and that God wanted action.

Everyone at the meeting nodded and then prayed in their own nutty way.

Then Sophia Alderson went through a list of possible options.

There was only one option she said which would actually stand any chance of working. It was the option both she and the Virgin Mother favoured.

A little while later a press conference was held at the gates of Rainthrope House. The four Popes read out a statement together on behalf of all those present at the meeting.

They called for a Holy War, a crusade against Scepticism Inc.

'It is time to end the obscene game Mr Malroy and his associates are playing at religious people's expense,' said the four Popes in near perfect harmony.

'This is something all holy people can agree on,' added Ayatollah Khorasani, who then urged all devout Muslims to take part in what he called the Jihad. 'Death to Scepticism Inc!' he shouted. Ayatollah Khorasani was so excited, jumping around and shouting 'Death to Scepticism Inc!' that his glasses nearly dropped off.

After Ayatollah Khorasani's performance the rest of the hundreds of religious leaders who had attended Sophia's meeting told reporters they were one hundred per cent behind the crusade.

The Holy War had started.

38

Rowdy crowds of priests, sages, witch doctors, shamans, gurus, soothsayers, healers and holy men attacked betting shops all over the planet. It was mayhem.

The ring of betting shops around the Vatican were seized almost immediately by Swiss Guards and the entire population of the Vatican City State, some seven thousand nuts, all of whom swarmed out of the main bronze door the moment the Holy War was declared.

?

Edgar watched events unfold from his office, as one by one the red lights representing betting shops on his almost three-dimensional map went out.

He was defiant. He said he had expected something like this all along. He was prepared. He gazed out at the horizon. He twiddled with his Geiger counter.

?

An hour after the Holy War officially began Edgar appeared on Who Knows TV. He sat on the sofa covered in question marks wearing his flak jacket and helmet and cradling a Chinese assault rifle. He smiled. He waved. He said Aloha. Then he said it had started. He said that any member of staff who wished to go home was free to do so. Those who wished to stay at their posts, to keep the betting shops open, had a right to defend themselves. Edgar had a sip of tea from the cup that balanced precariously on one of the arms of the sofa. Edgar told his audience that he had expected something like this would happen. He had been waiting for it. He said he had really been waiting for it all his life. He told his audience of nuts that he felt it was a fundamental right for a person to spend as much money as they liked on whatever metaphysical crap they subscribed to. Edgar said that he was prepared to die defending that right. Edgar promised that whatever happened he would always be willing to take nuts' money off them for things they couldn't prove. 'As long as there is a breath left in my lungs I will continue to write out receipts, I will continue to offer my services to all the nuts in the world. This I assure you. Edgar Malroy promises you: The show will go on.'

He asked his audience if they wanted their children to have the freedom to place metaphysical bets when they grew up.

Edgar drew a picture in his audience's minds of a world devoid of betting shops. 'Do you want that? Do you really want that? Is that the sort of future you want?' he asked.

It could happen at any moment. Sceptic Tower itself might fall, he warned. Who Knows TV might be taken off the air at any time. Pop. Just like that.

Edgar told his audience that this might be their last chance to place a metaphysical bet.

Edgar then looked at his watch and had another sip of tea.

Within the next quarter of an hour another forty-three million pounds worth of metaphysical bets were taken by Who Knows TV.

Another seventeen religions went to the wall as a result of the bets made in that quarter of an hour.

As Edgar pleaded successfully with his viewers to part with larger and larger sums of money, girls in white swimsuits and flak jackets with furry pink question marks on their heads, that waved to and fro, fought with hundreds of priests who had broken through the electrified fence around Sceptic Tower.

Back on Who Knows TV Edgar appealed to nuts to join in the defence of the betting shops. A bullet smashed a window in the Who Knows TV studio. Edgar switched the safety of his rifle off. 'Do you see what it's like down here? Do you?'

Three more bullets whizzed into the studio. A sound man was shot in the neck. Edgar's tea cup exploded. Edgar leapt behind the sofa and returned fire. His false eye fell out and rolled under the sofa. His helmet fell off. A tracer round hit the sofa and it began to smoulder. A technician came on screen with a fire extinguisher.

Edgar crawled around the front of the smoking sofa and pleaded with his audience to continue to bet whatever happened.

They did so like crazy.

It was wonderful TV.

Everything was used to repel the attacks on Sceptic Tower: chairs, tables, paperweights, boxes of metaphysical receipts were thrown from the tower onto the heads of the priests below.

As things deteriorated Edgar phoned the police. He told them he was under attack. The police said they would send someone around.

39

Fighting went on for days and days.

Somehow Edgar managed to visit, by helicopter, the handful of betting shops that were still open in and around London.

He would inspect the shops, climb onto a betting booth, normally with some assistance, and give what was intended to be a morale-boosting speech. He mumbled on about blind guesses and the raping of the world with words.

Then he would shout out his battle cry, which was this:

Who knows? Who fucking knows?

He said the same thing to reporters.

Edgar somehow found time during all this to go on giving us lectures at Who Knows College. Edgar's lectures during the Holy War took place underground in the boiler room because the upper levels of the college had been gutted by fire and every now and again were raked by machine guns. Edgar told us that religion was oppression. He said it was all designed to imprison us inside terrifying concepts.

He told us people with the Truth, with God on their side, were the saddest, funniest, scariest, dumbest things there were.

?

In the United States the President called out the National Guard to try and restore order by separating the combatants. Most of the National Guard simply took sides and fuelled the conflict.

The same thing happened all over the planet when governments ordered their soldiers and policemen to intervene in the Holy War.

Nearly all of the red lights on Edgar's almost three-dimensional map had, by this stage, gone out.

?

Those betting shops that remained open reported brisk business despite the fighting. Thousands and thousands of nuts went on betting even as priests took pot shots at them as they ran across no man's land with their chequebooks flapping in the wind.

It was sheer lunacy and Scepticism Inc.'s profits continued to grow.

As the death toll rose the United Nations Security Council called on both sides to show restraint. It even organised peace talks in Geneva.

No one showed up.

Sceptic Tower continued to hold out and Who Knows TV went on broadcasting and taking bets.

?

On the 19th of November the last of Scepticism Inc.'s great digging machines, intended to turn the deserts of the world into farmland, was finished. Edgar named it Sophia. Sophia was shipped on barges to Western Australia.

?

Edgar paid all his staff who were still alive overtime.

He was everywhere at once.

He led the defence of Sceptic Tower, he masterminded relief efforts for the handful of betting shops still open, he went on giving stirring speeches on the futility and madness of religion and shouting his battle cry. He continued to lecture us and he still appeared regularly on Who Knows TV, keeping his viewers updated on the fighting, telling them which shops were still open, which had temporarily ceased trading, and begging his audience to keep the bets coming.

On the 18th of November Who Knows College fell.

About thirty-five students, including myself, were evacuated from the college by white helicopters with question marks on their doors.

An hour earlier we had sat our exams. I had done rather well thanks to my ZEm 12000 Nexus memory system. Edgar himself had written my answers down for me.

We were taken to the relative safety of Sceptic Tower.

40

I worked on my dissertation with a girl in a white swimsuit in a room on the two hundredth floor of Sceptic Tower as the Holy War raged below us. My dissertation was entitled 'The Kernel of Truth' and was heavily influenced by Edgar's essay 'Why Religions Are Like Cereals' which he had written for Sophia Alderson some years before.

On the 20th of November 2026 Sophia Alderson, in combat fatigues, called on all Scepticism Inc. employees to lay down their arms and come out of their betting shops with their hands in front of them in prayer. She said further resistance was useless. She demanded Edgar cease all trading for the love of God.

Edgar responded to Sophia's ultimatum by showing his tattoo to the audience of Who Knows TV for a full ten minutes.

?

Another fifty-five religions died out. The main Tokyo Metaphysical Betting Shop fell to a combined assault by Shintoists, Buddhists, Crypto-Christians and New Mormons. Another sixty-three offices were lost in the US to priests of the Polish National Catholic Church in America, Pentecostals and Black Muslims.

The last betting shop in the whole of Mexico was surrounded by twelve bishops and five hundred preachers of the Union of Evangelical Independent Churches.

In London, Sceptic Tower continued to hold out against overwhelming odds.

?

In the deserts of the world Edgar's massive digging machines went on making kilometre-wide trenches and I finished my dissertation two hours before the deadline. Sceptic Tower was being attacked at the time I remember by an assortment of Roman Catholic priests, Rabbis, Brahmans, Witches and Druids.

Edgar was in the main lobby firing a heavy machine gun and mumbling Aloha repeatedly under his breath. He told me to leave my dissertation on his altar/desk.

It was then that a girl in a white swimsuit with a furry pink question mark on her head, carrying belts of ammunition over her shoulder for Edgar's machine gun, handed me a telegram.

It was from St Dr or Dr St Cunningham. It said simply:

WE MUST TALK.

41

As the Holy War raged another General Council was summoned to try and end the Second Great Schism. It failed abysmally, merely electing yet another Pope.

Dilipkumar Thanki, the sixteenth Dalai Lama, was elected Pope on the 3rd of December 2026.

The sixteenth Dalai Lama had secretly become a Catholic priest a month before.

By then some thirty-three per cent of organised religions had perished. The Holy War, which had cost the lives of some eighty-eight thousand Scepticism Inc. employees and an equal number of nuts, was not going as planned. Although Sophia and the other religious leaders were loath to admit it, their actions had only had a minor effect on Edgar's profits and thus their own financial difficulties. It was true that the number of walk-in bets had decreased since the start of the War by something like sixty-eight per cent, but the average amount of money put on individual bets had jumped tenfold. As long as Who Knows TV and Who Knows FM remained on the air Edgar would continue to threaten the very existence of all organised religions on the planet. Efforts to take Sceptic Tower were redoubled.

80mm mortars were used to shell the tower around the clock. The mortars came from Russia and had been blessed by every kind of priest you can imagine.

The blessed mortars were firing when I decided to try visiting Dr St or St Dr Cunningham by dashing across no man's land.

42

In the chaos I managed to push myself unmolested to Pentonville Prison with an hour of visiting time remaining.

Dr St or St Dr Cunningham was sitting in the visiting room wearing a grey prison uniform and a bright red bow tie and matching spectacles.

I said Aloha and he thanked me for coming. He asked me how the war was going.

'Who fucking knows?' I said.

Dr St or St Dr Cunningham said that he had something heavy weighing on his mind.

He went on to tell me that he had thought of little else since he had arrived in jail. At first he said he didn't want to believe it. He told himself his conclusion had to be wrong, but he couldn't deny the evidence. Every night he'd break out in cold sweats. At this point St Dr or Dr St Cunningham broke down. I tried to comfort him.

'You've been trying to explain your nutty belief in God, you've been trying to find a rational basis for your faith. I've been there, I know how it feels,' I said. 'I spent two years pushing myself up Everest trying to figure the whole thing out. Trust me, there isn't any proof of God. Its all a matter of blind faith. Metaphysical speculations are all – '

'This isn't about God.'

'No?'

'No.'

'Oh.'

'Sophia . . .'

'Sophia what?'

'She loves him.'

'Loves who?'

'Edgar.'

'No.'

'She mumbles his name in her sleep every night. I've been there when it's happened.'

'He mumbles her name in his sleep. He masturbates about her in his bathtub shaped like a question mark every night.'

There was silence. A prison guard coughed falsely.

Dr St or St Dr Cunningham pulled hard on his bow tie and looked down at the ground.

I didn't know what to say.

'To get them together would be sheer lunacy in my professional opinion. They're both too unstable, too – '

'But they love each other,' I said.

'Yes, I believe they do.'

'What a mess,' I said.

St Dr or Dr St Cunningham broke down. Again.

He pulled again on his bow tie. It came undone and the poor

man looked as despondent as it was possible to be. 'I love Sophia Alderson more than I can say,' he said. 'I know you think she's nuts and everything and I agree she is, but all that doesn't matter. I love her. From the day I was put in charge of her case I loved her.'

It was then that I confessed to Dr St or St Dr Cunningham something I had not told anyone before, not even Edgar. I told him as he fumbled with his bow tie that I had loved two women in my ridiculous life; one had been Kitty Fitzgerald who had introduced me to the universe and the other was Sophia Alderson who, a little while after the Great Mania, had her followers toss me onto a bonfire.

Dr St or St Dr Cunningham put his hand on my push-bar and said that he knew how I felt.

We regained our composure a little after that and discussed what we were going to do.

Together we devised a plan. A stupid, pathetic plan, that would end more horribly than either of us could imagine.

A plan that Dr St or St Dr Cunningham said in all honesty, with not a hint of irony, 'might just work'.

That night I slipped back into Sceptic Tower with more stealth and cunning than you would imagine a bent and buckled super-market trolley capable of.

?

A week later, after an early-morning attack had been repulsed, our graduation ceremony took place in the main lobby of Sceptic Tower.

Edgar congratulated us and asked, 'Who knows?'
    To which we replied: 'Search me!'

My fellow students and myself were then presented with our diplomas.

I would later have mine framed.

After that we all did the Errr and congratulated each other.

I will remember that day for as long as I live.

43

After being awarded my diploma I was flown to the very first Metaphysical Betting Shop to help take metaphysical bets.

I even got to wear a furry pink question mark on my push-bar.

I said Aloha to Edgar, not sure if I would ever see him alive again.

The first Metaphysical Betting Shop was not how I remembered it. Dead bodies littered the grass outside and barbed wire was everywhere. Fellow employees connected my direct feed interface to a computer terminal and I waited for my first customer. He did not take long to appear.

He was a middle-aged man in a track suit who bet £7,500 that Jesus Christ had a divine nature only, rather than a human and divine nature.

He was shot in the arm as he tried to leave.

My second customer was a fatalist. He bet £10,000 that what will happen will happen and nothing we do or do not do will make any difference. When he had made his bet he walked out the door not even bothering to duck.

After him an old lady somehow managed to reach the betting shop, wrote out a cheque for £500 and bet that there is an ineffable, radiant consciousness outside space and time and beyond subject/object distinction, which is realised with the stopping of conceptualisation.

What happened to her I don't know.

After that there was a lull in business as priests attacked the building.
    Bullets bouncing off the bulletproof stained-glass windows sounded like popcorn popping.

Time passed.

?

In all I took 2,323 bets.
    I took £120 for the bet that God is both personal and compassionate and is father and mother. I really did. I took £10,530 off a woman, her entire life savings she told me, for the bet that once freed from the attachment of the senses the soul may become fused with the universal spirit.
    I took £5,000 from a one-legged man for the bet that the behaviour of all living things is in part due to a life force which cannot possibly be explained by physics or chemistry.
    A man in pyjamas bet £6,000 that the incarnation of God in Jesus was impossible since all matter is evil. After him a man in a clown's outfit bet £500,000 that millions now living would never die.
    After each of the nuts made their bets they stood in the doorway and affixed their 'I've put my money where my metaphysics are' badges proudly on their chests and then rushed out to face their chances against the machine guns that were trained on the betting shop.

The whole thing was just terrible. Day after day I was forced to watch nuts disappearing into the sunlight. All I heard after that was the chatter chatter of the machine guns. How many of my customers escaped with their lives I can't say.

I even had regulars. Nuts who ran across no man's land every single day. One bet that God was protecting him so that he could keep on betting. He made the same bet every day. Then one day he failed to show.

Another nut spent a totally silly amount of money on the claim that God is one and that there is no unity that is in any way like his. He bet on this once a week.

At the end of March a nut was shot in the back just outside the betting shop. He threw a wad of money into the shop and after a few moments I asked him what he wanted to bet on. He couldn't make up his mind. First he said that he wanted to bet that Christ ascended into heaven and sits on the right hand side of God, then he said he wanted the money spent on the bet that Emmanuel Swedenborg had direct access, via dreams, to the spiritual world, then he changed his mind and said that he wanted to bet that the Roman Catholic Church has a divine right to prevent its members reading material harmful to their faith. The poor nut was slowly losing his mind. He asked me what I thought he should bet on.
    'Who knows?' I said.
    In the end the nut said he wanted to bet that the Bible was completely accurate and that the beep beep beep noise one heard on the radio just before the news was the voice of God.

He died soon after that.

Aloha.

44

Summer came and the Holy War went on and on.

I was taking money off a nut who believed that Marshall Herff Applewhite, leader of the Heaven's Gate cult, was God's messenger when it was reported on the news that Dr St or St Dr Cunningham had somehow escaped from Pentonville Prison.

I got one of the girls I worked with to phone Edgar. I told him to drop whatever he was doing and to pick me up.

He wanted to know what as going on. I told him to trust me.

An hour later a white helicopter landed on the grass next to the first betting shop. I was pulled aboard and the machine rose into the sky.

'Where are we going?' Edgar asked.

'Rainthrope House,' I told him.

Edgar was silent for a while then he said, 'Is that wise?'

'Trust me,' I said, and poor Edgar did just that.

He radioed back to Sceptic Tower informing them that he was flying to Rainthrope House. The employee on the other end of the radio said, 'Be careful out there.'

I had taken my last metaphysical bet.

So effectively had Edgar.

45

Sophia Alderson had stopped wearing combat fatigues.

She was in her room putting the finishing touches to her wedding dress. She had made it herself. It was made of wool. It made her itch terribly. She liked itching terribly, she thought it brought her closer to God. She looked in the mirror. She did her hair. Had St Dr or Dr St Cunningham or Edgar Malroy been in the observation room that day, they would have been utterly lost for words.

In the rose garden of Rainthrope House Pope Philips stood looking at his watch. Then he clapped his hands, and around the skinny pontiff rushed priests and choirboys carrying giant candles and crucifixes.

Sophia Alderson was about to be made a full-blown Carmelite nun. Her parents stood just inside the rose garden holding hands. They had been flown in for the occasion from Sicily where Sophia's father had become a very successful insurance salesman.

Outside the rose garden some two thousand heavily armed followers of Sophia Alderson stood patiently waiting to witness their spiritual leader become a fully-fledged nun. It was a very moving time for them; many were crying like billy-o already.

Behind the crowds of adoring followers, under a willow tree, was Pope Philips' piano, which had been flown in for the occasion from South America. Pope Philips' piano was being lovingly cleaned by one of Sophia's followers. Next to the piano was a very long table covered with thousands of glasses full of carrot juice.

After taking one last look at herself in the mirror Sophia Alderson lowered her veil and received her very last visitation from the Virgin Mary, who was dressed as a traffic warden. When Mary had gone, Sophia jumped into her wheelbarrow and was pushed out of her room by a nodding follower and gently bounced down the stairs. Her perfect bosom was undulating wonderfully.

Written on the Virgin Mary's placard was the very last message Sophia Alderson would ever receive from the Mother of Jesus. It went like this:

You look like a million dollars, kid.

When Sophia Alderson rolled into the sunlight a thousand hearts were broken and there was a collective sigh, as you might have expected.

For Sophia Alderson was as beautiful as the Tarantula Nebula seen in infra-red.

She was as beautiful as the stagnant pool out of which life arose.

She was as beautiful as all of George Milles Jr's wives put together.

She was as beautiful as beautiful can be.

Pope Philips looked at his watch again and said they really ought to get started. Sophia took the Pope's hand as he led her over to the gaggle of priests at one end of the rose garden. The massive candles were lit and hundreds of Sophia's followers bit their lower lips.

Pope Philips told Sophia to kneel. She did so in her wheelbarrow as elegantly as can be. She then placed her hands together in prayer.

Sophia's father took a series of photographs. Later he would discover that he had failed to put any film in the camera. He would be distraught.

Pope Philips coughed and then began to cross himself.

?

It was then that Dr St or St Dr Cunningham, riding a bicycle like a man possessed, pedalled into the grounds of Rainthrope House shouting for everyone to stop what they were doing. Behind Dr St or St Dr Cunningham were four police cars, their lights flashing.

When they saw the thousands of heavily armed followers of Sophia
Alderson standing there, the police sat in their cars and called for
back-up.

Dr St or St Dr Cunningham pedalled right into the rose garden
and then took a few minutes catching his breath. All he could
think to say was how beautiful Sophia looked.

Pope Philips, greatly put out, looked at his watch again.

Sophia stood up in her wheelbarrow. 'This is truly a miracle, St
Cunningham. God has seen to it that you are to be present at my
wedding to his only begotten son. We must pray in thanks. We
will pray together.'

'There isn't time, Sophia,' Dr St or St Dr Cunningham said
desperately, looking for something to tick.

'I agree,' said Pope Philips.

'Sophia, I have to ask you to do something,' said Dr St or St
Dr Cunningham, still a little out of breath.

'After I have been joined in holy matrimony with Christ.'

'No. It can't wait, you have to do it now.'

Everyone then heard the thump thump noise of a helicopter.

46

'Listen to me. God wants you all to turn around and put your
fingers in your ears. Wait! Before you put your fingers in your
ears let me tell you that God also wants you to count very slowly
to one thousand out loud. God has also made it very clear to me
that whatever happens you have to keep your backs turned and
keep counting. It is God's will. Who are you to argue with God?
OK now, turn around. Yes, you too, Mother.'

Sophia turned off her loudspeaker system. 'Now what was all
that in aid of?' she asked Dr St or St Dr Cunningham.

'Who knows?' he said.

Pope Philips demanded to know what was going on.

Then the Scepticism Inc. helicopter landed in the centre of the rose garden. Petals flew everywhere.

Sophia's wedding dress billowed like crazy and all the giant candles were blown out.

Edgar stepped rather nervously out of the helicopter.

Sophia fell out of her wheelbarrow. Dr St or St Dr Cunningham scooped her up.

None of Sophia's followers moved.

Edgar waved shyly at Sophia, said Hi, and then with the help of the pilot, who was chewing gum, removed me from the helicopter.

Pope Philips reached for an assault rifle, thanked God for his good fortune and levelled it at Edgar.

I told the Pope that there was no need to shoot Edgar as he was surrendering, unconditionally. Edgar didn't raise a whimper in protest. He hadn't heard me. He was still waving at Sophia.

The Pope stopped pointing the gun at Edgar Malroy and turned it instead on Edgar's pilot.

Pope Philips demanded to know if the pilot was chewing Popegum. The pilot swore that it wasn't Popegum but Pope Philips wasn't satisfied until he had been shown the screwed-up wrapper.

Sophia and Edgar kept on looking at each other.

Sophia's followers, their backs turned, kept on counting. They had got to sixty-eight.

234

'Say something to her,' I whispered into Edgar's ear.

'What?' Edgar said.

Pope Philips put down the gun, turned back to Sophia and clapped his hands. Sophia knelt down again in her wheelbarrow in front of the Pope. Every now and again though she kept glancing back at Edgar.

The giant candles were lit again and the Pope again made the sign of the cross.

It was then that the Popemobile smashed its way through the police cars that blocked the entrance to Rainthrope House and swerved into the rose garden, running over the feet of two of Pope Philips' priests and dousing everyone in holy water.

The holy water put out the holy candles and Sophia's wedding dress was ruined.

Edgar told me that she looked even more beautiful soaked. She did. Her impossibly long eyelashes looked like saw blades.

Although they were being doused in holy water Sophia Alderson's faithful followers continued counting, their backs turned, their fingers in their ears. They had got to 123.

The cockpit of the Popemobile opened and, undoing his World War I flying helmet, Pope Thanki, the former sixteenth Dalai Lama, leapt to the ground.

Pope Philips picked up his gun and pointed it at the other Pope and started shouting about how he was doing the ceremony and no one else and how he would have had it wrapped up hours ago if he wasn't being constantly interrupted. He also told the former Dalai Lama to turn the damn sprinklers off.

Pope Thanki said he didn't know how to turn his holy water sprinklers off, he was new at the controls. Then Pope Thanki asked if we had heard the news yet. Another General Council had been summoned near Sebastopol. The General Council had ten minutes ago excommunicated all of the Popes and elected a new one. The General Council had elected Sophia Alderson as Pope.

'I don't believe you,' said Pope Philips. Pope Thanki said it was perfectly true. 'Would a Pope lie please?'

Sophia didn't pay any attention to what the two other Popes were arguing about. She was staring at Edgar.

Pope Philips refused to believe Pope Thanki and insisted on continuing with the ceremony. Pope Thanki said that it was necessary to postpone the ceremony. He had two reasons for this, one was a matter of theology: could a Pope also be a nun? The second reason was that he really had to discuss urgently with Pope Alderson the possibility of ending the Second Great Schism.

Pope Philips was having none of it. He said that Pope Thanki would just have to wait until after she had been married to Christ. Pope Thanki threatened to excommunicate Pope Philips again. Pope Philips threatened him back.

I pushed Edgar forward.

'Say something to her,' I whispered.

'Don't rush me,' Edgar said.

Sophia knelt down in her wheelbarrow completely drenched in holy water. The wetter she got the more beautiful she became. Her angelic nipples began to show through her wedding dress.

A priest started trying to light the giant candles but Pope Philips told him to forget it. Pope Philips then crossed himself and began marrying Sophia Alderson to Jesus H. Christ of no fixed abode.

Edgar just stood there and told me how beautiful she looked.

Sophia's followers got to 250.

47

Sophia Alderson's followers got to 500.

Pope Philips got to the bit where Sophia was supposed to say 'I do' to a man who had died more than two millennia ago.

It was at that moment that Edgar's watch started to beep for the very last time.

This is what was on the liquid crystal display:

You are about to die

At the same moment the Popemobile's holy water tanks ran out of holy water and it stopped raining.

Edgar leapt into the space next to Sophia Alderson, the space supposedly occupied by an invisible Jesus Christ. Edgar said that he had something to tell Sophia, and pushed her off to the other end of the rose garden, holy water spilling over the sides of her wheelbarrow.

Pope Philips stood there for a while then looked at his watch and said, 'That's it. I give up!' and pushed his way through the followers of Sophia Alderson, making his way slowly to his piano that rested under the willow tree.

It was nearly four thirty in the afternoon. It was a beautiful sunny day.

?

Pope Philips had got about halfway to his piano when through the gates of Rainthrope House sped a security van.

The security van was going far too fast. It careered out of control and smashed into first Pope Philips' piano and then the willow tree.

As it disintegrated the piano made a most horrendous noise.

Sophia's followers, who had counted up to 635, didn't bat an eyelid.

The willow tree swayed to and fro for a while then crashed down onto the security van. Glasses of carrot juice went everywhere.

Pope Philips sank to his knees in disbelief.

The driver's door of the security van opened and out climbed the former Archbishop of Canterbury and Primate of all England, pushing aside the branches of the willow tree. He walked the short distance to Pope Philips.

He patted Pope Philips on the back. Pope Philips, still kneeling, his head cast to the ground, grunted.

The former archbishop then pushed his way through the crowd of Sophia Alderson's followers, and greeted Dr St or St Dr Cunningham, Pope Thanki and myself.

The girls at Sceptic Tower had told the former archbishop where Edgar was to be found. The former head of the Church of England wanted to make just one more metaphysical bet. He wanted Edgar to take the bet personally.

I don't know what Edgar said to Sophia Alderson before he told her the joke but both of them were laughing and smiling as he pushed her wheelbarrow around the various rose beds.

You wouldn't have been able to tell just by looking at the two of them that one was a nut and the other a nihilist evangelist, that the two of them disagreed fundamentally about everything. They just looked like a short man with a limp pushing a very very beautiful woman in a wheelbarrow around a rose garden in the grounds of a mental asylum that had been turned into the headquarters of a religious movement.

?

This is what happened next:
A bee began circling Edgar. Edgar shooed it away with his good arm. The bee then started to bother Sophia. The bee circled Sophia's utterly perfect little head. On the third lap, as Sophia's followers reached 867, the bee flew into Sophia Alderson's pretty little mouth.

It really did.

Sophia Alderson's pretty little mouth was open because she was laughing at the joke Edgar had just told her. It was the first joke I had ever heard. It was about wheelbarrows.

Sophia stopped laughing.

Edgar asked what was wrong. He thought that she was having a visitation or something.

The bee buzzed its way down Sophia's pretty little throat. Sophia gripped Edgar's hand as she felt the little bee buzz further and further into her.

The bee reached Sophia's beautiful little stomach and died almost instantly but not before it had stung Sophia in her windpipe.

Sophia really stopped laughing then and died of suffocation in Edgar's arms, her face the colour of a blackberry.

Sophia Alderson believed that the whole universe was built to a most wondrous plan and that everything that happened happened with a purpose.

Aloha.

48

Time passed.

Edgar shook Sophia.

More time passed.

Edgar rolled up his sleeves, mumbled something about porcelain and hit Sophia Alderson with his walking stick shaped like a question mark.

Pope Thanki and Pope Philips crossed themselves.

Sophia Alderson's beautiful jaw went pop.

Yet more time passed.

I didn't move.

Even more time passed. Edgar's walking stick broke and Dr St or St Dr Cunningham and the pilot carried Edgar to his helicopter which moments later took off in the direction of Sceptic Tower.

Pope Philips was next to the security van collecting piano keys. Pope Thanki stepped solemnly to the other end of the rose garden and said a few words over Sophia Alderson's body.

Sophia's parents and her followers went on counting, their fingers still in their ears.

Dr St or St Dr Cunningham ran his hand along my frame and very slowly went inside Rainthrope House.

I just stayed there in the rose garden for a bit listening to Pope Thanki mumble on about nothing. Pope Philips' priests and choirboys joined in.

The giant candles were relit.

As the wheelbarrow with Sophia's body in it was being pushed slowly around the rose garden by Pope Thanki, I pushed myself through the crowd of Sophia's followers and the policemen that were gathering nervously outside the gates of Rainthrope House and headed back to the first Metaphysical Betting Shop. The former Archbishop of Canterbury followed me with several gold bars in his hands.

The former archbishop plugged in my direct feed interface to a computer terminal and was just about to tell me what he wanted to bet on when the giant television hanging from the vaulted ceiling tuned to Who Knows TV went dead.

One moment metaphysical bets were running across the screen, and then the screen went blank.

Then there was the flash.

49

It was brilliant white. Unbelievably white.

'What was that?' said the former archbishop, dropping his gold bullion.

The bulletproof stained-glass windows imploded and the entire betting shop lurched to the left. Then gusts of wind rushed in from outside and it was like the worst days on Everest.

Far off on the horizon through the broken windows we could see Sceptic Tower. It was soaring into the sky. Climbing up and up into the air like a rocket, great chunks of it falling away as it rose. Huge oily clouds of red purple smoke seemed to be pushing it higher and higher.

The tower's ascent slowed as we watched, then it started to sway to and fro. It swayed like that for what seemed like an age then it toppled over and fell into the maelstrom below.

A vast mushroom cloud took shape where Sceptic Tower had been.

Thirty-eight thousand people were killed instantly.

The great dome of St Paul's was cracked like an egg and billions of metaphysical receipts flew out and filled the sky.

Eventually there were so many metaphysical receipts in the air that they blocked out the sun.

50

The bomb had been made of Red Mercury; mercury antimony oxide dissolved into mercury and then left to irradiate in a nuclear reactor for twenty days.

An hour after the explosion a Muslim group calling themselves Tanzim al-Jihad claimed responsibility.

At exactly the same time a shadowy Catholic movement known as the Bloody Cross also claimed responsibility.

Extremist Hindus told journalists they had planted the bomb, as did literally hundreds of followers of Sophia Alderson.

Six hours after the bombing eighty-two religious groups had claimed responsibility and the police were getting more calls all the time from groups swearing they had planted the bomb.

?

The billions of metaphysical receipts that littered London following the cracking of St Paul's dome were highly radioactive. People were advised not to have anything to do with them. Men in spacesuits collected them with pointed sticks.

?

The handful of Metaphysical Betting Shops that remained surrendered and the stock market crashed.

?

Dr St or St Dr Cunningham slipped out of the country and

surfaced in Papua New Guinea. He became in effect the leader of Sophia's followers. Dr St or St Dr Cunningham and some ten million nuts all over the world prayed to Sophia in heaven by the ticking of clipboards.

?

As for the Second Great Schism, well it went on and on, growing more and more out of control. Pope number six turned out to be a waxwork dummy, Pope number seven committed suicide, Pope number nine retired two days after being elected and became a contemporary dancer, Pope number ten had previously been a sheep shearer and Pope number eleven had been on death row in America. Twice.

?

I was five years old when Edgar died. He had been twenty-seven. He has a grave, although hardly anything of him was ever found. Scientists assured me that an atom or two of what had formerly been my best friend would be present in any pile of gravel from within the blast zone.

I had an MoD official in a spacesuit scoop up such a pile of gravel. We were then both sent through an army decontamination unit a number of times. The army decontamination unit was a borrowed automatic car wash.

Edgar's epitaph reads:

Not sleeping but dead.

EPILOGUE

A month after Edgar's death the United Nations granted my request to become a space probe. I was hastily placed aboard Space Shuttle Virile and put into low earth orbit. I think they were glad to get rid of me.

By the time I left the planet something like three hundred and eighty organisations had claimed responsibility for the bombing of Sceptic Tower.

From low earth orbit you could see Edgar's handiwork. Written in kilometre-wide trenches on the desert of the Sahara you could make out the following words: *Who Knows?*

The question mark hadn't been finished; it looked more like an exclamation mark. The tip of the question mark was to have reached the Red Sea but digging had stopped while there was still two hundred and fifty miles to go.

A few minutes later Space Shuttle Virile passed over North America and the Mojave Desert. It was possible to make out the letters: *Who Kn*

Again there was no water in the canals. We passed above each of the six great deserts of the world seeing clearly Edgar's canals and noting the absence of water.

In the desert of South America was the single word *Who*.

The Gobi desert had the letters *Wh*.

The Namib Desert had a massive *W* carved out of it and the Australian outback had a mark that looked like the letter *V*.

There was not a drop of water in any of them. Edgar's plan to turn the deserts of the world into farmland had failed. Religions flourished again and fifty million people went on dying of starvation every two years.

After we had orbited the planet a few times I was released from the cargo bay and sent in the rough direction of the star system Epsilon Eridani. At Cape Canaveral I had had rocket pods attached to my frame and a radio receiver/transmitter welded onto my push-bar. I used the rocket pods to adjust my trajectory. I would later use the radio receiver/transmitter to send this long and winding electromagnetic transmission.

Eight years after leaving Earth I left the solar system.

Aloha.

79,650 years later I reached the star system Epsilon Erdani with my framed degree in agnosticism.

304 Earth years ago I parked myself in high orbit around the fourth planet of the Epsilon Erdani system. I have named it, rather unimaginatively, Edgar's World.

The planet is ten thousand kilometres in diameter, one hundred and twenty million kilometres from its sun and its atmosphere, at a guess, is composed mostly of Aminomethyl propanol, the stuff used in many hair-styling products.

It looks quite beautiful.

I have every hope that in twenty billion years or so life will appear on this little world. When it does so, barring no mishaps, this life will evolve into people, as life does.

I will be able to talk with these people when they develop radio. (I cannot land on the planet, for I would burn up the moment I entered the atmosphere.)

*   *   *

I will have much to say to these people when they get here. I will tell them about Earth, about human beings and their civilisation. I will tell them about Art and Supermarkets.

And when they ask me about the purpose of life, as I'm sure they will, I will tell them about Edgar Malroy and what he would do whenever anyone asked him about the purpose of life.

No doubt these people will not find this answer very satisfactory and their priests will ask me about God etc etc. In reply I will send a very short message translated into whatever language these people will have invented for themselves. The message will be this:

Who Knows?

Aloha.

AUTHOR'S NOTE

Most of the names in this book are actually names of the Midland Bank's financial planning managers. A list of their names appeared in an advertisement in the Sunday *Observer* on the 4th of December 1997. The ad reads, 'I am Mike Lindup and I'm a little indisposed, but if you call 0800 65 65 65 one of my colleagues will be in touch.' Then the ad lists the names of all the Midland Bank's financial planning managers. You may have seen it.

There are eight hundred financial planning managers' names on the ad.

I have only used a few.

No offence intended.

Midland Bank plc is a member of IMRO.

Scepticism Inc. is in part about porcelain art at the end of the twentieth century. Porcelain art is rarely central to a work of prose and this novel should be seen as an attempt to rectify matters, at least in relation to porcelain art at the end of the twentieth century.

Here is the moral of the story (in case you missed it):

People matter more than The Truth.

A NOTE ON THE AUTHOR

Bo Fowler was born in 1971. He studied Philosophy at Bristol University before attending the University of East Anglia where he studied Creative Writing under Malcolm Bradbury. He is currently working on a PhD in Critical and Creative Writing. He intends to write one hundred novels and then die.